Reverdy Johnson

A Brave Soldier

A true patriot, a noble man, defended against partisan malice : reply of
Hon. Reverdy Johnson to the paper which Judge-Advocate Holt furnished
to the President, urging General Porter's condemnation

Reverdy Johnson

A Brave Soldier

*A true patriot, a noble man, defended against partisan malice : reply of Hon.
Reverdy Johnson to the paper which Judge-Advocate Holt furnished to the
President, urging General Porter's condemnation*

ISBN/EAN: 9783337309350

Printed in Europe, USA, Canada, Australia, Japan

Cover: Foto ©Raphael Reischuk / pixelio.de

More available books at **www.hansebooks.com**

A BRAVE SOLDIER, A TRUE PATRIOT, A NOBLE MAN

DEFENDED AGAINST PARTISAN MALICE.

REPLY

OF

Hon. REVERDY JOHNSON

TO THE PAPER WHICH JUDGE-ADVOCATE HOLT FURNISHED TO THE PRESIDENT, URGING GENERAL PORTER'S CONDEMNATION.

[It will be remembered by the public, that after the Court-Martial had made up their judgment and transmitted it to the President of the United States, Judge-Advocate-General Holt furnished to the President, without the knowledge of General Porter's Counsel, an argument in favor of condemning Porter. The able reply of Senator Johnson comes too late to save Porter from the cruel sentence inflicted on him, but not too late to save him in the hearts of his countrymen, who owe him all that a nation ever owed to a brave and faithful defender of her cause. It is a duty, in the performance of which all true Americans will unite, to give this document the widest possible circulation.—*New-York Publishers.*]

REPLY.

NOTE.—The references to the evidence, etc., are to the Record of the trial, as published by order of the House of Representatives.—EX. DOC. No. 71. Thirty-seventh Congress, third Session.

THE preparation of this Reply was delayed until a printed copy of the Record in the case of Major-General Fitz-John Porter was obtained, and since, by professional engagements, which the writer was not at liberty to set aside. It is now submitted in the confidence that the intelligent and impartial reader will coïncide in opinion with the writer, that a greater injustice was never done through the forms of a judicial proceeding, than was done by the sentence of the Court-Martial in the case of that gallant officer.

BALTIMORE, July, 1863.

To vindicate a citizen unjustly assailed, is the duty of all men who properly estimate the value of individual character and its influence on the public good. The duty is the more imperative, if the services of such citizen have contributed to the honor of his country, and have been rendered with great toil and solicitude, and amidst frequent and imminent perils. To this general obligation in the instance which causes this paper, there is with the writer superinduced the special one growing out of the professional relation in which he has heretofore stood to the officer whose case forms its subject. His first personal acquaintance with Major-General Fitz-John Porter was, when he became one of his counsel on his recent trial. Before then, he knew him only, (and who did not so know him who has followed the history of our sad civil war?) as a patriotic, skillful and gallant officer, giving his days and nights to duty, ever discharging it to its fullest measure, and on all occasions answering the highest expectations of his superior officers, his friends and country. In his hands the military service had not only suffered no dishonor, but had attained even higher distinction. He had achieved for himself a name of which the nation was justly proud, and a reputation amongst all those of his brothers in arms, who, being themselves worthy of their noble profession, saw, without envy, every manifestation of his skill and gallantry, and rejoiced at it as enhancing the reputation of the service, and giving the assurance that a patriotic soldiery led, as Porter led his men, could not fail to extinguish the rebellion, restore the people to their former happiness and prosperity, reïnstate the Government in its rightful authority, and give it a name with the nations of the world, even brighter and more commanding than it had ever possessed. The high esteem in which, in common with all, the writer held Porter, was, if possible, increased after he became his counsel. And to that esteem was then soon added the closer and even stronger ties of personal friendship. For weeks, seeing him constantly, not only in the Court by whom his case was tried, but in private consultation, he had every opportunity of becoming acquainted with the man, and as far as he is capable of judging, with the officer. He witnessed in the former that freedom from vanity, that mildness of disposition with that firmness of purpose which are often united, and a strong sense of honor that won for him his highest regard, and in the latter a devotion to his profession, a perfect acquaintance with all the conflicts in which he had been engaged, a cheerful readiness in rendering honor where honor was due, a mildness of censure where he thought errors had been committed, an ardent love of country, and a confident consciousness of innocence of the charges which he was to answer, which, independent of all other evidence, satisfied him that such charges were in every particular wholly unfounded.

When the evidence was all given, he regrets to be compelled to say, that he was further satisfied that they were as malicious as unfounded. But, though then, and still so convinced, he would never have deemed it necessary to bring his case again before the public in the form of a vindication, notwithstanding the sentence of the Court affirming their truth, but for the reasons he is about to give. A defense was made before the sentence was pronounced, and by all who heard it, or who have since read it, a defense considered as triumphant and unanswerable. So universal was this opinion, that when the evidence and the defense had been seen, an acquittal was anticipated with undoubting confidence. So great and general was that confidence, that never in the history of jurisprudence, civil, criminal, or military, was a judgment announced that so shocked and startled the sense of public justice. In speaking of the ability of the defense, the undersigned but pays a just tribute to his associate counsel, Mr. Charles Eames, by whom it was, in every thing deserving praise, exclusively prepared. But what occurred without the knowledge of General Porter, or his counsel, whilst the case was progressing, and in the Court, whilst the evidence was being given, and at the close of the reading of the defense, and what has since occurred has rendered it proper, in the opinion of the writer, that the public judgment should be again invoked. Upon various grounds, it is not less due to Porter, and to truth—than to the good of the military service, and to the confidence so material to that good which is to be placed in future military judgments, that the attention of the public mind should be once more invited. The grounds referred to are these:

I. Pending the trial, the evidence of three of the leading witnesses of the prosecution, Major-General Pope, Brigadier-General Roberts, and Lieutenant-Colonel Thomas C. H. Smith, was secretly and anonymously published in Washington, in pamphlet form, with a title-page which, as evidently intended, would lead the reader to suppose that it contained either all the evidence in the case, or that the evidence that it did contain was in no particular rebutted by other proof. Porter has since discovered that the cost of this publication was paid by Smith, and that Roberts transmitted copies to persons in several of the Northern States, and as believed, to many members of the Senate of the United States, a fact disclosed in part in a short debate in that body at its recent session. On a motion calling for the Record for the purpose of publication—Mr. Fessenden objected, because, as he stated, the Record had already been printed, a copy of it having been sent to him, (by whom sent he did not say, because he did not know,) but doubtless by Roberts, or by his direction. Even by so discerning a gentleman and accomplished a lawyer as Fessenden, the fraud of the publication was not discovered.

II. The rulings of the Court, (which for obvious reasons could not be commented upon in the defense,) on questions of the admissibility of evidence in some instances, and as the undersigned believes in all, were so palpably erroneous, and so injurious to Porter, that they foreshadowed in colors too striking to be mistaken, the result to which a majority of the Court would arrive. These errors were so apparent as to excite the surprise, and incur the censure, as the writer knew at the time, of distinguished Judges, and members of the bar without an exception, unless the Judge-Advocate was one. It is not meant to say that he was, especially as on more than one occasion, he himself intimated the error and induced the Court to correct it.

III. When the evidence was all introduced, the counsel of Porter requested to have until the following Monday to prepare the defense, but the Court suggested, because of other pressing engagements of some of the members, the following Saturday. This suggestion was agreed to by the counsel with the understanding, sanctioned by the Court, that if the Judge-Advocate replied, the counsel should have the right to rejoin. Whether he would reply or not, that officer declined to say. The Court was then cleared, no one remaining with them but the Judge-Advocate. The evidence was, it is said, read over, doubtless commented upon by all, and from the celerity with which the sentence followed the reading of the defense, even charity can not but believe, that it was determined upon before a word of the defense was heard. The defense was read on Saturday, the tenth of January, 1863, and the moment it was concluded, which was about half-past two o'clock P.M., the Judge-Advocate said, orally, that he did not propose to answer it, but that he submitted the case on the part of the Government without remark. The Court was then cleared, the Judge-Advocate again remaining with them, and before six o'clock P.M., the sentence pronounced, that the accused "be cashiered," and "be forever disqualified from holding any office under the Government of the United States." The character of the evidence, as published from day to day in the journals of the country, had so satisfied the public of Porter's innocence, and that conviction become the more fixed and absolute when it was seen that the Judge-Advocate declined to answer the defense, thereby seemingly submitting to a judgment by default, and that the Court decided so immediately after the defense was closed, that all saw it was impossible, even that the evidence could have been read, much less so considered as is due to proper judgment, or the defense either read or compared with the evidence, a measure called for by judicial propriety and necessary to a just and enlightened conclusion. In this state of the public opinion, as manifested by the concurrent voice of the entire press, that spoke at all, the record was placed in the hands of the President. Unless he had before been unofficially advised of it, he must, when he read the sentence, have been struck with the same surprise with which its after announcement struck the public ear. Of all the men in the country, he must have experienced not only astonishment, but concern. In May, 1861, he had commissioned Porter a Colonel in the regular army, in August of the same year, a Brigadier-General of volunteers, and in July, 1862, and for distinguished services in the Peninsular campaign, a Brevet-Brigadier-General in the regular army, and a Major-General of volunteers. Honors due to him, in the view of the President, for amongst others, the services rendered to his country in the battle of Malvern, a battle which, in the words of his Chief, McClellan, in a letter to the President written just afterward, and near the battle-ground, and speaking, as he said, "not from hearsay, but from personal observation," that had eclipsed, "in its result any other engagement in the campaign," and that too much credit could not "be

given to General Porter for his skill and gallantry on the occasion."

The President, then, could not but have paused before approving such a sentence, and asked himself how it was possible that Porter, the idol of his men, the boast of the army, the pride of his chief, and the recipient of honors which, from a sense of public justice and gratitude, he had conferred upon him for distinguished and valuable services rendered his country in a most perilous crisis, should all at once have been so recreant to his past patriotism, so forgetful of his then well-earned and universally acknowledged fame, as to have committed acts almost before the ink was dry upon the parchments containing his commissions, and whilst the public heart was so gladdened by his deeds of skill and daring, as to demand, in the judgment of a Court composed of brother officers, that he "be cashiered," and "forever disqualified from holding any office of trust or profit under the Government of the United States."

The Record was of great volume. As published by Congress, inclusive of the defense, it consists of two hundred and ninety-eight closely printed octavo pages. The President should have taken time, before approving of such a sentence, the writer respectfully submits, to have examined it to find what it could contain to justify such a judgment. The mere sentence itself gave him no such information. It was, as is usual, but a mere naked judgment, and must, therefore, have left his mind in the condition of amazement in which it could not but have placed him. Nor could he discover why, if at all, his distinguished Judge-Advocate should have sanctioned such a result. The Record contained no reasons of that officer, summary or in detail. It did contain the defense of the accused, and if he had read that, his amazement could but have been increased, as he would have seen that it was, what all but the Court, or to speak (as there is reason to believe) more accurately, a bare majority, thought a complete and perfect vindication. The President's time, however, was perhaps so engrossed by matters which he supposed to be of more pressing national moment, (as if any thing was more important than justice,) that it was impossible, within the period, the twelfth of January, 1863, when the Record was placed in his hands, and his approval of the sentence promulgated on the twenty-first of that month, that he could have read it through carefully, or at all, or examined the testimony, or tested the fairness or sufficiency of the defense, by an accurate or critical review of the evidence. Nor, as it now appears, did he undertake what, in the interval referred to, would have been an impracticable task. For, as is stated in the review of the Judge-Advocate, which it is the main purpose of the writer to answer, on the thirteenth day of January, 1863, the day after the Record was transmitted to him, the President issued "written instructions" to that officer, "to revise the proceedings of the Court-Martial in the case of Major-General Fitz-John Porter, and to report fully upon any legal questions that may have arisen in them, and upon the bearing of the testimony in reference to the charges and specifications exhibited against the accused, and upon which he was tried." These instructions produced an elaborate paper, dated the nineteenth of the same month. The Record between that day and the date of the instructions, and the prior thirteenth, must have been continuously in the exclusive possession of the Judge-Advocate. It is probable that the Record, with the review, was not returned to the President before the twentieth, but, however that may be, it could not have been returned at the earliest sooner than the day of the date of the review, the nineteenth, and on the twenty-first the sentence was approved. It is even, therefore, the more obvious than it would otherwise be, that in this short period of two days, proper examination and comparison of the proofs, and the bringing to their test Porter's defense, and subjecting to the same test the Judge-Advocate's review, (each vital to a proper consideration and just conclusion,) could not have been made by the President. The inference, therefore, is irresistible, that in this instance at least, (with motives which his established character prevents our questioning, how much we may lament its weakness and injustice,) he has rested his judgment, though severely calculated to dishonor a well-tried public servant whom he had but recently before, over and over again, honored by acts of distinguished official favor, upon the argument of his Judge-Advocate alone, without collating it even with the portions of the evidence quoted by that officer, much less with all the evidence so material to understand properly and justly the portions quoted, or even stopping to discover what is thought to be quite apparent, the depth of the prejudice which that officer entertained toward the accused. Reposing, however, confidence in the Judge-Advocate, he has, yielding to the pressure of other engagements, submitted his own judgment to the keeping of that officer. And he did this so entirely, that it does not seem to have occurred to him, that it was in any respect due to Porter that he should have an opportunity, through his counsel, of replying to the argument of the Judge-Advocate. What occurred in the Court on that point could not, therefore, have been made known to him. He could not have been told, that in the view of the Court, if a reply was made to the defense, it was due to the accused, and his privilege, that he should have the right to rejoin. But it is most singular, and not to be accounted for, except that his other harassing and important engagements deadened his sense of justice, that a right so justly due to Porter, and so necessary to truth, had not suggested itself to his honest mind, and more especially, as his long experience as a lawyer must have taught him its importance.

But so it was. The accused then, as far as the President's action is concerned, has had his case decided on the argument of the Judge-Advocate's review, not only without having had accorded to him the privilege of reply, but without the President's having taken time to read all the evidence, if he read any part of it, or to read the defense, or to test that or the review by comparing either with the whole evidence or with any part of it. The rule of military law as laid down by Sir Charles J. Napier, is now well settled, that no matter how many addresses are made by either party, "the prisoner has the right to speak last." *Bennet*, pp. 123, 124. In this instance, the rule was grossly violated. The last speech was made by the Judge-Advocate. Porter was not only not permitted to reply, but the existence even of the review was apparently concealed from him, certainly was not known by him until in common with all, after the sentence was announced, approved and circulated by the War Department. To any mind accustomed to the investigation of truth and the ascertainment of facts through human testimony, such means are known not only to be important but essential. No conclusion arrived at in any other way, can be relied upon. No judgment, otherwise formed, is entitled to the least respect. In any instance it is as likely to be wrong as right, and more likely to be wrong, in a case where it affects injuriously the character of a citizen whose antecedents had challenged not only the good opinion of those who knew him, but their admiration, and whose claim to public esteem rests on admitted valuable and perilous public service. In such a case, mental imbecility or prejudice, so deep and dark as wholly to cloud reason, must be supposed to be the foundation of the error. And with an evident consciousness that the observing and correct mind of the country would be astounded at the result, with a zeal and industry worthy of a better cause, the same resort, which so evidently misled the President, has been adopted to quiet the certainly anticipated public condemnation. While the Senate refused to call for the Record in order to its publication, (because of their having been deceived through the degrading artifice of Roberts and Smith, into the belief that it had all been published,) that the people might see the whole case, the review of the Judge-Advocate was at once published at the expense of the War Department, and scattered broad-cast over the land. Other things, too, have happened, suggestive of most unpleasant reflections — reflections casting more than a doubt on the mere abstract correctness of the Court's sentence. Almost simultaneously with its publication, three of the members of the Court were made Major-Generals, all certainly most estimable gentlemen, and possibly competent soldiers, but with no claims to such promotion. One of them, Major-General Prentiss, the only one of the three who it is confidently believed, did not concur in the sentence, has recently proved himself worthy of his rank, by his skilful defense of Helena, Arkansas. But the public in vain at the time, endeavored to recollect any fact as to either calling for such an honor, and have not been more successful since, except and very recently as to Prentiss. And they have asked, and still ask, if their distinguished services and the good of the country required their elevation to such high rank, why was it not conferred before? And why, why above all, was it the immediate sequence of the sentence against Porter? Who can answer satisfactorily either question? None certainly has as yet come from any quarter. The President of the Court, Major-General Hunter, was also immediately returned to a command from which he had been shortly before removed for acts of alleged mistaken policy, or excess of authority, and from which it has been found necessary to remove him a second time.

Of the three witnesses, Major-General Pope was continued in an important command, notwithstanding his sad failure in his Virginia campaign. Brigadier-General Roberts was assigned to a more important one than he had ever held before, or to which any competent officer who had known him believed him equal—nor in his career since has he done any thing to attract attention, except in the way in which his former chief signalized the commencement of his Virginia career, the issuing of proclamations as uncalled for as they were ridiculous and futile. It has also been found necessary in his case, to take it from him, and he is now once more on Pope's staff.

What disposition has been made of Lieutenant-Colonel Smith, is not known, and probably no one cares. (Appendix, No. 5, p. 86.) He perhaps continues to be one of the military family of Pope, ready whenever his exigencies may require it, to display for his benefit, the extraordinary faculty which he claims to possess—the reading of souls at first sight. The faculty of receiving, to use his own words, an "impression," although unable to analyze it from a few moments' intercourse with another—the power to obtain "one of those convictions that a man has a few times, perhaps, in his life, (he is modest enough not to claim to have it always at his command,) as to the character and purposes of a person who he sees for the first time," and although "no man can express altogether how such an impression is gained from looks and manner, but it is clear."

Under all these circumstances, with every ingenious mind, a sentence announced as this was, would be without the slightest authority, and no reason could exist for subjecting it to serious examination. The fact, however, that the present one is maintained and justified by Mr. Judge-Advocate-General Holt, makes it in a measure advisable. The well-established reputation of that officer, his perfect loyalty, his eminent ability, and the somewhat plausible character of the review, considered by itself, seems to require that that review be answered. For, however, as the writer has good reasons for believing, this is thought to be unnecessary by those who have made themselves acquainted with all the evidence, there must be a numerous class of citizens, who not having done so, may have been led astray by it.

The ingenuity of the Judge-Advocate, and his deservedly high reputation, gives to it an authority to which it will be seen it is not entitled, when it comes to be examined. A reader uninformed as to the evidence, will be unable to detect his sophistry or discover his prejudice, a prejudice doubtless unknown to himself, but not the less strong, and perhaps stronger on that account. Under this impression, it is the purpose of the writer to subject the review to the ordeal of reason and of truth. This he feels to be not less due to Major-General Porter, than to the good of the service, and the benefit of the country. An officer, whose deeds on so many battle-fields in the present war have so enhanced the nation's fame, filling with gratitude the very "pulse and veins of the people," whose patriotism from the first, was not only never before called into doubt, but admitted, and signally honored and rewarded, should not be permitted to suffer in the estimation of one honest citizen from a paper, whatever of high character may belong to its author.

There are further considerations, which, in the judgment of the writer, call for an answer. Before the sentence was made public and since, Porter has been assailed, with a bitterness implying malignity as well as ignorance, and by a few persons filling high official places, and whose claim to capacity and confidence, (however ridiculous these are to those who know them,) may have misled a part of the public. Amongst those are some who pretend to be military critics. Possibly themselves led astray by their own turgid conceit, they may believe that they possess this highest of intellectual powers. And where they are not self-deluded, their blatant patriotism (ever the art of the demagogue) may possibly mislead the unsuspecting. These last are slow to believe that such pretenders to knowledge and virtue can design to delude. Their assumed wisdom for a time is taken at its nominal, not its real worth—their judgments, valued at their author's estimate, and not at their actual value. And for a period, miraculous even as it may appear, they are supposed to be infallible judges of military subjects, to be men whom nature has made chosen objects of her favor, imparting to them the faculty of mastering military science without either study or practice, although in all other respects they are seen to be placed low in the scale of human capacity. It is consequently possible that to some extent these pretenders may have given to the sentence of the Court some little sanction. This furnishes a further reason for the vindication of Porter, and to these several reasons, perhaps, is to be added yet another. It is not to be disguised that in the conduct of this sad war, different views of policy have been entertained in the army as well as in Congress. The resolution adopted in 1861, with so much unanimity by that body, declaring what the object of the Government in the war was, was approved with almost the same unanimity by the army, men as well as officers, and by the people. That policy, then so generally approved, has been since departed from, whether wisely or not it is not the writer's present design to inquire. The chief authors of the change have from the first charged almost every military disaster and the failure of a complete triumph over the rebellion to the want of concurrence in the wisdom and propriety of the change in a portion of our military leaders, and have literally clamored for their removal. To this class Porter was supposed to belong.

Whether he did or not the writer has no certain knowledge, though he thinks it probable, as by nature and intelligent patriotism he is conservative and national. But to suspect him of not changing his individual opinion as Congress changed its own, in the estimate of the men alluded to, was fault enough. In their view every officer whose opinions were supposed to be the same on certain subjects as those of McClellan and Porter, and who has failed to abandon them at party bidding, has been continuously assailed with the same bitterness. Even the present Commander-in-Chief is constantly subjected to its fury. Assaults are made upon him from day to day, and with ever increasing violence. His removal is demanded under the pretext of the public good, but really to gratify party purposes. His capacity is denied—his patriotism questioned, and the Presidential ear literally dinned with the ignorant and false clamor. Thus far, however, it has been without avail. His having abandoned his distant home on the Pacific, where every comfort surrounded him, and no peril threatened or could come, purely from a sense of patriotic duty to serve the country in the present crisis, and his having subsequently on the field and in the closet given his days and nights to her assistance, all avail nothing. These voracious hawkers after objects of party sacrifice seem literally to gloat, and with no concealed delight, over any officer, (the higher he stands in the public esteem the greater the pleasure,) who they think they can make a victim to their thirst for victims to promote party success.

Porter, too, was known to be a personal friend and admirer of McClellan. He had every means of judging of McClellan's capacity, of witnessing his love of country—his constant efforts to serve her, and his military skill and genius, and the result was, that he highly appreciated him as a citizen and an officer. And this, in the view of the men referred to, seemed to be almost if not fully as great an offense as treason. He became therefore at once an object of vituperation, and no efforts were spared to shake the confidence that the President had so conspicuously placed in him. When Pope's disgraceful failure was evidently stirring the public mind to the folly and injustice of taking from McClellan the command of the army of the Potomac, and arresting his plan of further campaign, it became apparently vital to party success that some safety-valve should be found for the harmless escape of the impending indignation. And it was thought that it would be found by ascribing that failure to treasonable conduct on the part of Porter, and this was done. A willing instrument for the purpose, Pope was supposed to be. It is but justice to that officer to say, that when he discovered it, he declined the degrading task. The charges at first were said to be his—he promptly disavowed them. That occurring, an informer was found in Roberts. The result is the dismissal of Porter from the service, whose fame he had so signally enhanced, and its being hailed with delight by the class referred to. Had Porter pursued a different course; had he, with the readiness of a mere party politician, regardless of his former opinions, adopted with instant and proclaimed zeal, those which Congress, forgetting their former opinions, afterward adopted; and especially, had he, oblivious of the teachings of his life, of his good name and honor, and of the opinion of the enlightened and patriotic, proved himself an inordinate braggart, boasted of his own merits, detracted from McClellan's, and stated that he, commanding the army, Richmond would long since have been ours—he, too, would doubtless now not only be in the service, but be the favorite and boast of the very men who have denounced him, and probably have been placed at its head. The rank ignorance of such men, their lofty pretensions, and supercilious arrogance, from its very extravagance, is in a measure captivating. Sublimity is at times found in the excess of the ridiculous. "An avenue of colossal toads might become sublime."

With these remarks, pertinent as the writer thinks to his purpose, he proceeds to answer the Judge-Advocate, and with all the brevity consistent with necessary fullness and perspicuity.

Evidently sensible of the insufficiency of the evidence considered by itself, and perhaps more sensible, that the President would so view it, to affect the accused in the matters charged against him, the Judge-Advocate devotes four pages of the thirty of his review to discover what had been the ANIMUS of the accused. To quote his language: "As the *animus* of the accused toward his Commanding General in pursuing the line of conduct alleged against him, must largely affect the question of his criminality, and may furnish a safe and valuable light for your guidance," (he is addressing the President, not the Court,) "in determining points, *otherwise left doubtful* by the evidence, it is proper that it should be ascertained before entering at large upon the review of the case, which you have instructed me to make."

What an exordium to a paper designed to induce a sanction of a judgment, dishonoring an officer whose life had been passed in faithfully discharging his duty to his country—whose loyalty and efficiency after the rebellion broke out, had been manifested in part under the orders of the reviewer himself, when he was at the head of the War Department, and to his entire satisfaction, and conspicuously displayed in the midst of great difficulties and peril, and whose conduct in the many battles in which he had been engaged, had excited the public admiration, and received the signal approval of the President.

The evidence alone, says the reviewer, is not sufficient to convict the accused, or to use his own words, his guilt is "*left doubtful by the evidence.*"

His *animus*, however, "may furnish a safe and reliable light," by which to discover his guilt. It may enable the President to determine what is otherwise doubtful. You must in this way supply, he tells the President, the deficiency in the proof. You must probe the mind of the accused. That may remove the darkness—furnish the light—explain the doubt. And to this, and with an earnestness that evinces a burning desire of success, he addresses himself with poetic license—with a beautiful though somewhat extravagant fancy, which, however it may please the ear, in the judgment of the wise, is a very unsafe guide to truth.

Not content with the asserted tendency of the telegrams, which he had offered in evidence to establish the so much wished

for ANIMUS, "Lieutenant-Colonel Thomas C. H. Smith, an Aid-de-Camp in the staff of General Pope," is resorted to for the charitable purpose.

His power to see into the very hearts of men at a single and first interview of a few minutes' duration only, preceded by no prior acquaintance whatever, is, and with a confidence which under other circumstances would, by a plain judgment, be considered simply ridiculous, seriously relied upon. The defense had characterized what this witness had said in regard to it, (and as the impartial and intelligent reader will think justly,) as "ravings, wild fantasies, rubbish, which should not have been suffered to encumber the Record."

How unjust this is, says the Judge-Advocate. "The witness (he says) endeavored to lay bare the foundations on which his belief of the accused's meditated treachery rested." He said that the manner of the accused "was sneering throughout, whenever allusion was made to matters connected with General Pope, and to quote his words, "his look was that of a man having a crime on his mind." But the Judge-Advocate admits, that the task (discovering with the only opportunity which he had the state of Porter's mind) "was a difficult one, and may not have been *entirely successful.*"

In other words, he admits that in this Smith may have failed, and done the accused injustice. He adds that "it was physically impossible for the witness to reproduce the manner, the tone of voice, and the expression of the eye, and the play of the features, which may have so much influenced his judgment. Yet these often afford a language more to be relied on than that of the lips. He could not hold up before the Court, for its inspection and appreciation, the sneer of which he spoke. And yet we know that a sneer is as palpable to the mental, as a smile is to the natural vision. It is a life-long experience that souls read each other, and that there are intercommunings of spirits through instrumentalities which, while defying all human analysis, nevertheless completely command the homage of human faith. Great crimes, too, like great virtues, often reveal themselves to a close observer of character and conduct, as unmistakably as a flower-garden announces its presence by the odors it breathes upon the air." From these quotations, the reader will see how vital, in the judgment of the Judge-Advocate, to the success of his palpable purpose to have the sentence approved, it was that the alleged criminal *animus* of Porter should be made out. Nor can he also fail to discover that, even with the reviewer's evident desire to discover it—his belief in spiritual "intercommunings"—his tendency to be led into error by his own imagination—his doctrine that the face often speaks the mind as unmistakably as the presence of a flower-garden is announced "by the odors it breathes upon the air"—he admits that in this instance the professor of the art, his lauded Lieutenant Colonel, "may not have been entirely successful."

He concedes that he may have misconceived " the look;" although, if the treachery " was then contemplated, it must be admitted as altogether probable that the shadow of such a crime struggling into being would have made itself manifest."

It is evident that the Judge-Advocate is not satisfied with the result of his search, so far, for the much wished criminal *animus* of the accused. A philosophic poet has said that there are occasions when—

"Thought meets thought ere from the lips it part,
And each warm wish springs mutual from the heart."

But to this, common feelings and a reciprocal nature are necessary.

Who that knows Porter, and has seen Lieutenant-Colonel Smith, could for a moment believe that such was their relative condition? Well might the reviewer, then, fear that his effort to establish, by such proof, the intended treachery of the accused, had failed. Well might he be sensible that such a task was even beyond his great powers, displayed either in imagination, spiritualism or argument. All exerted together for such an end, could not lift folly to respectability—make absurdity reason—a ridiculous pretense plausible, or for a moment with a considerate, honest, and unprejudiced judgment, injuriously affect a soldier, who, with fearless intrepidity and consummate and applauded skill, had so faithfully served his country, at a period when so many had proved faithless. In addition to the strong impediment which was thus interposed to the success of the Judge-Advocate's purpose, there was another. The witness himself, in addition to the nonsense already referred to, proved that he was not in this particular, at least, to be relied upon. He was so bewildered with his own conceited flummery, that if he is to be believed, it was near making him the greatest of criminals. He told the Court what the Judge-Advocate omits to inform the President, that on his return to his chief, after his ten minutes' interview with Porter, he stated to the former: "I was so certain that Fitz-John Porter was a traitor, that I would shoot him that night, so far as any crime before God was concerned, if the law would allow me to do it." What an avowal, almost a boast. That the laws of man alone restrained him, not the laws of God, from committing murder. And yet, this witness with this horrible avowal fresh in his mind, the Judge-Advocate tells the President, is " a man of fine intelligence," " that his *conscientiousness* rendered him careful, and guarded in his statements, and that he evinced a depth and solemnity of conviction, rarely paralleled in judicial proceedings."

What mind, but one so blinded by prejudice, that its light was for a time extinguished, would not, on the contrary, at once and with indignation, have rejected the testimony of such a witness, even if its transparent doltishness was less conspicuous. But prejudice jaundices the finest as well as the weakest intellect, and makes every thing appear of its own color. To immaterial facts and idle fancies, it attaches substance and reality. It affects the very warp and woof of the mind, engenders suspicion, and gives to idle and trivial circumstances, the weight of unanswerable proofs. He who read through all hearts, and knew and described man in his loftiest exhibition of virtue—his grandest of crime, and his lowest of weaknesses, says jealousy (and in this it resembles prejudice) is one of his frailties. "Trifles, light as air, are to the jealous, confirmation strong as proofs of holy writ," and " shapes faults that are not."

These observations are not made in any unkind spirit toward the Judge-Advocate. His talents are admired, and his public services and patriotic virtue in this epoch of our history, have given him an honored place in the grateful heart of the nation. But this renders it the more important, when his great authority is used to justify the sentence against Porter, a soldier to whom the country is yet more indebted, that that authority should be examined, that it may be taken only at its intrinsic, and not at its adventitious worth. If it has been depreciated by what has been already said, such depreciation can not but impair it throughout, and cause the reader to receive with more than doubt all that it urges against Porter.

Notwithstanding his evident foregone conclusion of the guilt of Porter, and his belief that to establish it to the satisfaction of the dullest and least charitable, it was most important to make good the hypothesis of his antecedent meditated treachery, and not satisfied that what were properly characterized as the "ravings and wild fantasies" of Lieutenant-Colonel Smith, would have that effect, he seeks to accomplish the end by resorting to certain telegrams, sent from time to time, during the campaign, by Porter to General Burnside. Some of these are in part given, and as the reader will see, most unjustly applied. Porter reported to Pope in writing, on the twenty-sixth, and in person on the twenty-seventh of August, '62. He had left Burnside, (under whose command he had been for some days before,) and he was requested by that officer to inform him from time to time by telegraph, how matters progressed. This request was virtually an order, and so considered, and acted upon by both officers. General Burnside said that he regarded sending the dispatches to him by Porter, "as an official act done by him in the performance of his duty," under his "direction." But this, says the Judge-Advocate, (p. 180,) "so far as the purpose for which they were offered by the Government is concerned, it is wholly immaterial under whose prompting, or *for what end* they were written."

Not for what end? However important to the public good the information they gave was—however patriotic the motive, the sending of the dispatches was immaterial in an inquiry as to the guilty or innocent purpose of the *animus* of the accused in the sending of them. They were offered by the Government to prove that Porter, at the time, "entertained feelings of contempt and hostility toward the army of Virginia, at its commander," and, "it matters not whether in a private and confidential, or in an official communication." So reasons the Judge-Advocate. Besides its shallowness, which of itself condemns it, he does not inform the President that they were sent under orders, or of what was proved by Burnside and others, though both facts were most important to enable the President to pass understandingly upon the case, *that every fact communicated by the dispatches was true.* Burnside was asked by the Court, "From what you know now, have you any reason to believe that the information given by General Porter in these telegrams, (meaning all that were sent to him,) as to the actual state of the army under General Pope, was not correct?" and he answered: "I *am myself quite satisfied that it was correct.*" "But that opinion is merely one based upon the information I then received, and what I have since heard." (P. 184.) And the Government offered no evidence to prove that they were not correct to the letter. Nor does the Judge-Advocate give the President, nor allude to it in any part of his review, the benefit of General Burnside's opinion, formed on these dispatches, as well as on his whole intercourse with and knowledge of Porter, that from the first, and to the period when he testified, he, Burnside, was satisfied that he would *prove, and had proved, true to his duty, to Pope and the country.* This is, too, the more surprising, as his very first question to Burnside discovers that he considered his opinion important. Could he have obtained the one he desired, would he not have used it, and even with more confidence than he uses the supposed "intercommunings of spirits," to show that Porter meditated treachery? His question was: "Will you state whether at the time these dispatches were received from General Porter, (say between twenty-sixth and twenty-ninth of August inclusive,) any of them excited in your mind the apprehension that General Porter might not be inclined to do his whole duty as a subordinate under General Pope?" The answer was: "I RECEIVED NO SUCH IMPRESSION AS THAT FROM THE DISPATCHES. *I saw in General Porter's dispatches exactly what*

I heard expressed by a large portion of the officers with whom I happened to be in communication at the time, a very great lack of confidence in the management of the campaign. It was not confined to General Porter. I saw in his dispatches and I told General Porter himself so, what may have been indiscreet language; BUT NOTHING THAT LED ME, FOR ONE MOMENT, TO FEEL THAT HE WOULD NOT DO HIS WHOLE DUTY." (P. 181.)

This evidence (could it have been by design?) was not only not given to the President, but its existence was not even intimated, although the Judge-Advocate was instructed by the President "to report fully upon the bearing of the testimony (the whole, of course) in reference to the charges and specifications," upon which Porter was tried. Neither was the President informed that, in answering the question by the Court, (the one already quoted,) which was intended, if possible, to find out whether Porter went under the command of General Pope with unfavorable impressions towards that officer, or whether such "impressions were gained after he was on the ground," the same witness testified : "He moved his troops off rapidly, and marched them at night, and every thing within my limits appeared to me to indicate that he was DETERMINED TO GET HIS TROOPS UP THERE AS RAPIDLY AS POSSIBLE. I SAW NOTHING TO INDICATE THE REVERSE," (p. 182.) Nor was the President advised that Burnside had testified, that in departing from an order of General McClellan as to the movement of his command from the Peninsula, and when it was known that they were to go to the aid of Pope, Porter was enabled to accelerate the movement—in the words of the witness, " to embark that much sooner and send the transports back for others," (p. 184.) Nor, finally, was the President informed that, in answering a question of the accused, the same witness had said, "I have never seen any thing to lead me to think that he (the accused) was ANY THING BUT A FAITHFUL AND LOYAL OFFICER;" nor that, in his opinion, every officer who knew him, and had witnessed his conduct throughout the war, as well as when he was under Pope's command, expressed, and in the strongest terms, PERFECT CONCURRENCE IN THIS OPINION.

General McClellan, under whose special eye he had served in council and on the field, so spoke of him. He said that from the time Porter "knew he was to go to the assistance of General Pope," he did, in his opinion, do "all that an energetic, and zealous, and patriotic officer could have done," (page 196.)

But the opinions of sensible men—men of well-known character, intelligence, and patriotism—seem to have been considered by the Judge-Advocate light as air, when contrasted with those of Smith and Roberts. The former, he appears to have thought, possessed but the ordinary means nature furnishes ordinary men to form opinions, whilst to one, of the latter, at least, Smith, she had supplied "instrumentalities which, while defying all human analysis, nevertheless completely command the homage of human faith," and as to Roberts, his well-known and universally acknowledged character for perfect veracity, almost chronic love of truth and spotless reputation with his brother officers, placed his evidence and the sincerity of his opinions beyond all possible suspicion.

That a chivalrous officer, whose life had been given to his country, and who but recently had so added to the reputation of its flag, should be sacrificed to reasoning so repugnant to common-sense that the unprejudiced mind rejects it at once as an insult to its intelligence, is one of the many extraordinary occurrences which, during the present rebellion, has so astounded the public. What but intellect perverted, could claim, as is done, for treason, the nobleness of patriotism—for oaths violated, the character of virtue—for rebellion, the justification of an absurd theory, or of an oppression that existed nowhere but in a diseased fancy? And what adds, if that be possible, to the injustice of the use attempted to be made of these dispatches, and so strongly indicates a predetermined conclusion against Porter, is the fact that, although stated to be offered to establish his alleged contemplated treachery, the Judge-Advocate objected to Porter's giving in evidence other dispatches to General Burnside a few days before and after the twenty-sixth and twenty-ninth of August, (the dates of those offered by the Government,) that is, from the twenty-second of August to the first of September, to disprove the alleged purpose, the *animus.* Strange as it may seem, the objection was sustained by the Court, and the proof rejected. A protest was entered. (See Appendix I.) That protest was published in the papers of the day, and in a short period the Court and the Judge-Advocate saw that the ruling of the Court was received with astonishment and disapprobation by the intelligent press of the country. Clearly illegal as the decision was, and strange as it is that it did not so appear to the Judge-Advocate and the Court at the first, they adhered to it until the manifestation of public opinion on the subject caused him to suggest the waiving of his objection, and the Court to admit the evidence. The dispatches were then received, but no one, aware of the circumstances under which they were received, believed that, however conclusive they were in disproving the alleged criminal intent or *animus*, they would have the slightest effect with the Court or the Judge-Advocate. The result proved that in this opinion there was no error. Nor does the Judge-Advocate, in his review, even notice them. The only reference he makes to them is to a single one of these dispatches which Porter desired to send, and was not permitted to send, to Major-General McClellan, dated second of September, 1862, and that one is not given at length ; and, although admitted to be "full of fervent patriotism and professions of devotion to his duty in connection with the Army of Virginia and its commander," the Judge-Advocate adds that, "unhappily it came too late." The merest trifle, which a fair mind would exclude as evidence of charges of dishonor and treachery against any one, much less a soldier, even before esteemed, is seized upon with avidity and tortured, or sought to be tortured, inconsistent as the effort is with common-sense, into proof of guilt, whilst the weightiest facts, those which, with such a mind, would be conclusive of innocence, for the most part are not mentioned at all, or when in part referred to, are rejected as unimportant, or as coming "too late." The President, however, should have been told of them, and the public should see the nature of the facts so discarded as not proving, or hardly as tending to prove, Porter's innocence of purpose. The Judge-Advocate, even in regard to the dispatches which he uses as establishing, in his view, the guilty purpose, omits to give the whole of any one of them. He extracts a few expressions from each, without alluding to its context, a practice ever unfair and unreliable. Had even the whole of these dispatches been disclosed, the President would have seen, and the public, for whom the review of the Judge-Advocate was also designed, as proved by its general circulation by the War Department, that these dispatches themselves proved no faithlessness on Porter's part to Pope or the country, either actual or contemplated. Whilst those which he does not give at all, or even allude to, with the exception of the one just mentioned, to McClellan, of second September, all demonstrate a fixed purpose and earnest solicitude to do his full duty to both. (The reader will find these dispatches in pp. 228–235.) It is confidently asserted that every one of them evinces not only a mere willingness, but the strongest wish to do every thing in his power to render the campaign successful, or, failing in that, to lessen, as far as possible, any disaster that might befall it, and especially to save the Capitol. His orders, too, to his corps commanders, to be found in the same pages, evidence intelligence, zeal, and energy, and the dispatch referred to, to McClellan, of second September, whilst he was still under the command of Pope, and involved in his fate, breathes the same patriotic spirit. That dispatch was an answer to one from McClellan of the day before, urging him "and all friends" to give "the fullest and most cordial coöperation to General Pope." A dispatch written, as McClellan states, (p. 197,) at the instance of and to satisfy the apprehensions of the President, and not to remove any apprehensions of his own. To quote McClellan's words: "I had no doubt then in my own mind but that the Army of the Potomac, and all connected with it, would do their duty without there being any necessity for any action on my part." To that message, Porter's of the second says: "YOU MAY REST ASSURED THAT ALL YOUR FRIENDS, AS WELL AS EVERY LOVER OF HIS COUNTRY, WILL EVER GIVE, AS THEY HAVE GIVEN, TO GENERAL POPE, THEIR CORDIAL CO-OPERA-

TION AND CONSTANT SUPPORT IN THE EXE-
CUTION OF ALL ORDERS AND PLANS. OUR
KILLED AND WOUNDED AND ENFEEBLED
TROOPS ATTEST OUR DEVOTION TO DUTY."
So conscious was Porter of having fully
performed his duty, the moment he received McClellan's dispatch he sought
Pope, showed it to him, and asked : " Why
he supposed such a dispatch had been sent
to him ?" (p. 20.) Pope could give him
no explanation. His answer to McClellan
he was not allowed to send, but it clearly
evinces the utter groundlessness of suspicion. His " killed and wounded and
enfeebled troops" he points to, as he well
might, as the witnesses of duty devotedly
performed. Of his command, gallantly
led by himself (for he ever led it) in the
battle of the thirtieth of August, three
days before, in a vain effort to turn the
tide of Pope's defeat, and, save the honor
of our flag, consisting of about seven
thousand men, he lost in killed and
wounded OVER TWO THOUSAND AND THIRTY-
TWO, INCLUDING IN THE KILLED ONE
HUNDRED AND FIFTEEN OFFICERS. All
this, however, in the view of the Judge-
Advocate, was " too late"—gallantry too
tardily displayed—wounds and deaths
proving nothing, patriotism and sense of
duty speaking but for the day, and not an
hour before. The twenty-seventh, twenty-
eighth, and twenty-ninth of August found
him a traitor in fact, as well as intent.
The thirtieth, a noble soldier and patriot !
And yet, with the transparent injustice
of such reasoning, the Judge-Advocate,
without seeming to be aware of it and of
its absurdity, tells the President and the
country, in concluding his review, that
" the Court was careful to give to the
accused the benefit of all well-founded
doubts that arose in their minds in reference
either to the fact of disobedience or in
reference to the measure of criminality
that prompted it, and hence found him not
guilty of the fourth and fifth specifications
of the first charge ;" and that, in the same
spirit of generous clemency, he himself
withdrew " the fourth specification of the
second charge," (p. 317.)
And this statement is seriously made,
without even intimating that in the support
of the specifications of the first charge to
which he refers, there was not only no
evidence offered by the Government, but

that what it did give, without considering
what was produced by the accused, established the utter groundlessness of both;
and without informing the President that
the specification of the second charge,
which he claims credit for having gene-
rously withdrawn, related to Porter's conduct in the very battle of the thirtieth or
August, where, under his lead, the battle-
ground was literally mired with the blood
of his devoted followers, and where his
efforts were so greatly instrumental in
diminishing the disaster of the day.
Having thus, it is confidently submitted,
shown not only that there is no proof to
establish the alleged criminal *animus* of
Porter, but conclusive evidence to the
contrary, the assumption of which *animus*
constitutes the very foundation of the
argument of the Judge-Advocate, the
charges and specifications will be considered in their order, and in connection
with the whole evidence.

FIRST CHARGE—FIRST SPECIFICATION.

The first charge was the " Violation of
the Ninth Article of War," and the first
specification, a failure to obey the following
order of Major-General Pope, dated " Bristow Station, August twenty-seventh, 1862,
half-past six P.M., Major-General F. J.
Porter, Warrenton Junction :"

" GENERAL : The Major-General Commanding directs that you start at one
o'clock to-night, and come forward with
your whole corps, or such part of it as is
with you, so as to be here by daylight to-
morrow morning. Hooker has had a very
severe action with the enemy, with a loss
of about three hundred killed and wounded.
The enemy has been *driven back*, but *is
retiring* along the railroad. We must
drive. him from' Manassas, and clear the
country between that place and Gainesville, where General McDowell is. If
Morell has not joined you, send word to
him to push forward immediately ; also
send word to Banks to hurry forward with
all speed, to take your place at Warrenton
Junction. It is necessary, on all accounts,
that you should be here by daylight. I
send an officer with this dispatch who will
conduct you to this place. Be sure to
send word to Banks, who is on the road
from Fayetteville, probably in the direc-

tion of Bealton. Say to Banks, also, that he had best run back the railroad trains to this side of Cedar Run. If he is not with you, write him to that effect.

"P. S.—If Banks is not at Warrenton Junction, leave a regiment of infantry and two pieces of artillery, as a guard till he comes up, with instructions to follow you immediately. If Banks is not at the Junction, instruct Colonel Cleary to run the trains back to this side of Cedar Run, and post a regiment and section of artillery with it."

The Judge-Advocate devotes five pages of his review to maintain this specification. With what justice, we will now see:

First.—The order was to bring by the specified time, "daylight," the following morning, not a *part* merely, but his "whole corps," or the whole of "such part as is with you." Porter had artillery with him, an arm of vital moment, at the time, to the accomplishment of Pope's purpose, and to the safety of his own command. This part of his force, too, the body of his order clearly embraced.

And if that could be doubted, the postscript made it clear. For in the postscript he was told that, in the event of his not finding *Banks* "at Warrenton Junction," he was to "leave a regiment of infantry and two *pieces of artillery*, as a guard until he comes up, with instructions to follow," that is, to follow with his own and these two pieces. The *artillery* of Porter was, therefore, manifestly included in the order. No part of that arm was to be left behind, except in the contingency mentioned, and then only two guns, and but for a time. On this fact, the Judge-Advocate is *silent*, although its significance is most important. The order exacted the movement of Porter's entire force, and embraced, in words, his artillery. To have left that behind, would have been disobedience; and if any untoward result had ensued to his own command or to Pope's, he should, and no doubt would, have been held responsible. Nearly all the witnesses proved that the artillery could not have been moved at one o'clock. In this part of the case, and indeed throughout, the prejudice of the Judge-Advocate reveals itself. After relying, and illogically and uncharitably

using the portion of the evidence which he quotes, as bearing on the question involved in this specification, he tells the President, "That there are certain other facts disclosed in the testimony, which go far to indicate a settled purpose on the part of the accused to disregard" the order. On receiving it, he said to the Generals who were with him, "There is something for you to sleep upon," instead of telling them what the Judge-Advocate, in his enthusiasm, says he should have told them, though he fails to say what that was.

Conceding that what he did say is correctly given, one would suppose that if it did not for a moment excite the surprise of the officers to whom it was addressed, (and against whom no fault of motive or want of skill is attributed, and all of whom are now faithfully serving their country,) officers who knew the actual condition of things, and saw the manner and heard the tone in which Porter spoke, an unprejudiced mind would find in that fact alone, ample confutation of the imputation, and dismiss, as wholly unjust and uncharitable, all suspicious speculations that could be founded upon it.

But Porter did not say what is stated by the Judge-Advocate. The reliable proof is the other way. What he did say was not in any degree "saddening or discouraging" to the officers who heard it, or to those who believe "that in the prosecution of this war, much vigor is much wisdom." In that maxim no one more decidedly concurs than Porter himself. This is evidenced by his whole conduct since the war commenced. What he did say, on reading the order to his Generals, was proved by General Butterfield, one of those present at the time. That officer states, that as soon as Porter received the order, he handed it "to General Morell, or to General Sykes, who were present, and said there was a *chance for a short nap*, or something of that sort, (I do not remember the exact words,) *indicating that there was but little time for preparation.*" And the same witness further stated, that on objections being made by Sykes or Morell, or both, to marching at one A.M., (they both testified that they did so object,) Porter stated what the Judge-Advocate neither gives or alludes to: "In reply to these remarks, *General Porter spoke rather decidedly, that there was the order — it must be obeyed; that those who gave the order knew whether the necessities of the case would warrant the exertions that had to be made to comply with it.* I do not state that as his exact words, but as the substance of what he said." (P. 185.)

What evidence is this of want of vigor, or of a purpose to disobey? No wonder that neither Sykes, Morell, nor Butterfield saw in it nothing to regret—nothing indicating a purpose or a willingness to disobey the order. Nothing "to the last degree saddening or discouraging for those who believe that in the prosecution of this war much vigor is much wisdom." Nothing sad or discouraging at all, but on the contrary, an ardent desire to obey the order. The Judge-Advocate, however, though *he* heard not the words, nor the tone, nor saw "the expression of the eye and the play of the features," which he tells us "often afford a language more to be relied on than that of the lips," (p. 301,) ruminating in his study, and even without a Smith, or any other expert in the reading of "the intercommunings of spirits," to supply his own possible want of information, and, with assumed confidence, construes them to have been most sad and discouraging, and to have exhibited nothing of "vigor," or of "wisdom." Can this be reconciled with his well-known ability, except upon the ground of his fixed antecedent hypothesis of Porter's guilt?

I. But to the evidence.

The order was received, as admitted by the Judge-Advocate, between half-past nine and ten o'clock of the evening of the twenty-seventh of August. The Generals who were present, Morell, Sykes and Butterfield, all say it was about ten o'clock.

II. When was the march under the order begun?

The Judge-Advocate says, it was not until about dawn. To make that statement good, he quotes a sentence or two from the testimony of a few witnesses. But why not all that these witnesses said? And especially why not have given the evidence of the Generals, who were present when the order was received, and

had charge of the movement, and of that of General Griffin, Lieutenant-Colonel Locke, Captains Martin and Montieth, and Lieutenant Weld? In fairness, it is obvious that this should have been done. General Morell was asked, "about what time did the march or movement of troops commence," and answered, "*at three o'clock, or very near that time.* That was the hour designated." (P. 145.)

General Butterfield (by Presidential appointment the chief of General Hooker's staff, whilst he was in command of the army) says, that General Porter fixed three o'clock as the hour, and that the witness "wrote an order in General Porter's tent, for my command to be in line to march at *three o'clock.*" And in reply to the question, "Did you march or attempt to march at three o'clock?" said, "*I did;*" "I had my column formed and staff-officers sent out to notify me where the head of my column should take its place in the line. We marched from the camp up to the road, and there waited until we could take our place, which was at the rear of General Morell's division." (Pp. 185, 186.) General Griffin, said: "I received an order about twelve o'clock on the night of the twenty-seventh of August, to move my brigade at three o'clock in the morning. *At three o'clock in the morning* I started from my camp toward Bristow Station, and marched about a mile or two, to where I halted, and there I remained at the head of my column until about two hours after daylight." (Why this delay he satisfactorily explains.) (Pp. 160, 161.)

Lieutenant-Colonel Locke being asked, "Did the corps march at three o'clock?" answered, "yes." (P. 134.) Captain Montieth: "At what time that morning did General Porter begin to move his troops?" "I should think it was *about* three o'clock." (P. 127.) And such is the testimony of all the witnesses upon this point, in fact of all who had the best opportunities of knowing, including the Generals whose duty, to move at three o'clock, under the order they all say they received from General Porter the night before, it was to see that that order was obeyed, and to superintend the movement. How idle it is to disregard all of this evidence as unreliable, and to find a fact inconsistent with it upon such testimony, little, too, as that is to which the Judge-Advocate refers, and of that little to General Pope's, who was not present at the time, who, to an inquiry, "Whether on the receipt of certain messages from the accused, the latter was on his march, in obedience to the order of the twenty-seventh of August," answered, "I do not know that he was. On the contrary, from a note I had received from him, (not however, produced, as were none of Porter's notes to this witness, who said that he had mislaid them all,) I did not understand that he would march until daylight in the morning." A story at war with the fact, that he had ordered the march to commence at three, and, as proved by the witness just referred to, that it did commence at that hour.

But, independent of the positive proof as to the time of the march, and supposing that the mind could possibly doubt upon the point with that proof before it, what are the probabilities? Every General and other officer present when the order was received, or who was in Porter's tent afterward on that evening, tells us that Porter gave a positive order to march at *three o'clock*.

If not obeyed, these Generals, who had to execute the order, were liable to censure. Who censures them? Not the Government, certainly. For, as before stated, and fortunately for the country, they are all of them in high favor. Porter is the only victim. He alone has been sacrificed, or rather as far as his reputation is concerned, a futile effort has been made to sacrifice him.

III. But admitting that he did begin his march at three A.M., the Judge-Advocate maintains that he was guilty of disobedience, meriting the sentence of the Court, because he should have marched, or attempted to march at one A.M.

However positive in that respect the order was, it was confidently stated in the defense, upon the authority of a military maxim of Napoleon, that passive obedience to a military order is only exacted "where it is given by a superior who is present on the spot at the moment when he gives it." The authority of this maxim is not disputed by the Judge-Advocate—he only denies

its application in this instance. And he does this but doubtingly. "Nor is it *believed*" (says he) that the accused can "find shelter" under it. And why—can the reader imagine? because, as this official military jurist says: "The discretion it allows to a subordinate, separated from his superior officer, is *understood* to relate to the *means*, and not to the *end* of an order. When the accused determined that instead of starting at one o'clock he would start at three or four, (he adds an hour, for all agreed that Porter ordered the march to begin at three,) he did not resolve he would arrive at Bristow Station by daylight in a different manner from that indicated by his Commanding General, but that he would not arrive there by daylight at all. In regard to this, the end of the order, he had no discretion." (P. 360.)

What technicality! A just and enlightened Judge once said of a like display in in a case before him, "it is stretching technicality to the very verge of quibbling."

A few observations will show the weakness of the reasoning of the Judge-Advocate.

I. In the first place, no such qualification of the maxim is anywhere suggested by its great author. His language is general, comprehensive of end as well as means. Passive obedience to an order in any particular, whether of end or means, is not to be exacted when the superior who gives it is not present at the place where it is to be executed. In the words of Napoleon, such obedience is to be exacted "*only* when it is given by a superior who is present on the spot at the moment when he gives it." And, as was his wont, he assigns succinctly, but clearly, the reasons for the rule. Having then, (that is, when he is present on the spot,) knowledge of the state of things, he can listen to the objections, "and give the necessary explanations to him who should execute the order." This, of course, he can not do when he is not present. To enforce absolute obedience to an order given by a superior who is not present, and may not know the condition of the country, or the difficulties in the way of its execution, might at times lead to the most disastrous results—imperil a corps, frustrate the very purpose of the superior, and so far from aiding, lead to his utter defeat.

II. What authority, other than his own, is there for his statement, that the maxim "is understood to relate to the means and not to the end of an order"? He cites none. Would he not, if he had known of one? And would he not have known if there be one? He shows himself to be fond of military literature, and to have its leading points fastened in his memory. He graphically calls to the President's recollection, the stirring scenes of Hohen Linden—the great gallantry and matchless energy of Richpanse—the dashing onset of Ney, and unites his own tribute to that of the renowned historian of *The Consulate and the Empire* to the consummate skill of Moreau, as being illustrated more brilliantly than in any of his other battles in this, "the greatest in the present century." Who can doubt that a mind which so evidently delights in military reading, and whose office of Judge-Advocate-General makes it his duty to do all that he can to master the science, as far, at least, as concerns obedience to orders, could have failed to discover in what authority, great or small, it is stated, that the quoted maxim of Napoleon was understood by him or any one else, military man or not, to relate "to the means and not the end of an order"?

III. But conceding, for a moment, that such is its meaning, how does that meaning deprive Porter of the benefit of the maxim?

I. It is said by the Judge-Advocate, that "the end of the order was that Porter should be with his command at Bristow Station by daylight the following morning."

II. That Porter did not decide to get there at that time, "in a different manner from that indicated by the order, but that he would not get there at all, at that time, and that as to get there at that time, was "the end of the order, he had no discretion upon the subject." Was the end of the order as suggested? The end must be the object to be accomplished by the order. The order stated that "Hooker has had a very severe action, with the enemy, with a loss of about three hundred men killed and wounded. The enemy has been driven back, but is retiring along the railroad; we must drive him from Manassas, and clear the country between that place and Gainesville, where General McDowell is." To clear this portion of the country then was Pope's object. He issued the order with that view. As a means to effect it he desired Porter's corps. In what condition? In fighting condition. In what way to get to him? By the best and shortest way. Time was important, but time was to yield to the object to be accomplished. Pope did not, and could not, know what would be the condition of Porter's command when the order would be received. He did not fully, if at all, know the condition of the roads, nor what would be the character of the night. In his designation of the time of arrival at Bristow's Station, did he mean to say, that no matter in what plight the troops should be—how far they may have marched that day and evening—what meals they may have had—what rest—what the state of the roads—what the character of the night, and what the opinion of every officer of the command as to the practicability of getting to Bristow Station at daylight— did he mean that, regardless of all these considerations, the order was to be literally obeyed? He did not, and could not have been supposed by Porter to have so meant, except on the supposition that he was an imbecile. The character for intelligence of Pope, therefore, should save him from the damaging effect of such a proposition. But in fact that was not his meaning. His conduct, the next day, when the troops did arrive at the designated place, which he says was twenty minutes past ten A.M., (Porter was, in fact, there about eight A.M.,) (p. 19,) proves, that he was guilty of no such folly. His order, according to the view, adopted by the Court and by the Judge-Advocate, had been shamelessly disobeyed. He had every reason, that view assumes, to know that it might have been obeyed. That Porter should be there at daylight with his command, was, it is said, the very end of the order.

That end had failed without justification or excuse, says the Judge-Advocate. If so, how are we to account for the manner of Pope's reception of Porter at eight o'clock that morning, or at any time after the command arrived? On cross-examination, Pope was asked: "Had you any conversation with him (Porter) in relation to the order of the twenty-seventh, and his having obeyed or disobeyed and if so, what?" He answered: "I do not remember any conversation with him in reference to obeying or disobeying the order, although I had much conversation with him." In replying to another question, requesting him to try and refresh his recollection, he said: "I should not be likely to complain to my subordinate officer of a disobedience to my orders, (why, he does not explain except that Porter was his subordinate,) I AM THEREFORE VERY SURE THAT I DID NOT COMPLAIN TO GENERAL PORTER." He added: "I am not sure that he gave me any explanations. I have a general recollection that he spoke to me of *his march, and the difficulties that he had in getting wagons out of the road, but the particulars I do not remember,* for I was very much occupied, and the necessity which made his presence important, had passed away." (P. 18.) On his examination also, in chief by the Judge-Advocate, he was asked: "Did he (Porter,) at that time, (the time of his arrival,) or at any time before," "explain to you the reason why he did not obey the order?" He answered: "He wrote me a note which I received I think in the morning of the twenty-eighth, very early in the morning, perhaps a little before daylight. I am not quite sure about the time. The note I have mislaid (as before stated, he said that he had mislaid all of Porter's notes to him—strange negligence this, and one that credulity itself could scarcely believe, if the witness's character for veracity and his repugnance to exaggeration, either delicate or gorgeous, was not so universally acknowledged.) I can give the substance. I remember the *reasons given* by General Porter; if it is necessary to state them, I can do so." Porter inquired if the witness had looked for the note, and he said he had, "but had not been able to find it." The Judge-Advocate then, although the inquiry *was his own,* and Porter *said* "*I do not object*" to the witness giving his recollection of the contents of the notes, said: "I will not press the question." (P. 13.) It appears then, that Pope had received before daylight on the twenty-eighth, from Porter a written note,

giving his reasons why he would not be able to execute his order literally. He sent no answer reiterating the order, nor did he rebuke, or in any way find fault with the failure in its passive obedience. And when Porter and himself met face to face, at eight A.M., and afterward on that day, also during the whole time, when Porter was under his command, and the whole subject was spoken of between them, and the difficulties of the actual march explained, did a single word, as Pope testifies, escape him, even faintly murmuring regret, much less censure! This of itself is conclusive of the groundlessness of the charge. The officer who gave the order, when he was made acquainted with all the circumstances attending its execution found no fault. Defeat had not then given his pride of command a sore wound. His ambition he no doubt thought would yet be gratified. He had at the time, Porter and his command with him, and he trusted, as he well might, to both, and by his own conduct at that time, it is demonstrable that he never intended to charge Porter with disobedience to that order. His doing so was obviously an after-thought. Defeat and not success was soon his fate. Defeat, great, overwhelming defeat. The public were indignant. If the result could not be attributed to Pope, (and that it could be it is not necessary here to charge,) the getters up of the campaign as well as Pope, impelled by natural mortification, looked for escape from the censure which they were certain to receive, to any victim that could with the slightest probability be found, and Porter was selected. His conduct, his disobedience, his meditated treachery were at once alleged to be the cause of the defeat. His telegrams were searched and criticised, his conversations hunted up and examined, and each expression, howsoever made or to whomsoever made, evincing a want of confidence in Pope's skill and capacity for the command, were seized upon and pressed into the service. Whilst it is known that some desired his life, the Court satisfied itself by displacing him from the army, and idly assuming to disfranchise him from all places of honor and trust under the Government. And yet, who in his senses concurs in the justice of that sentence, or fails to stamp it as a gross wrong to Porter and the country? For a time he may not again be permitted to honor his profession, and serve the nation by other deeds of skill and valor, but of the past he is not deprived. The place in the hearts of his fellow-citizens, which he filled after his crowning achievement of Malvern, is his still. And soon will the people order those, who, as they should do, *will* listen to the public voice, and be alive to the public honor, that he must be restored to their service, and afforded an opportunity of adding, if that be possible, to his own reputation, and to the military renown of the nation.

But to return to the evidence. It is true that to a certain extent he criticised in his dispatches to Burnside, the plans of his chief. As he did it, was it a crime in any view, military or otherwise? His criticisms were for the eyes of Burnside only, and of those of the President and Commander-in-Chief, to whom he must have known they would be communicated. If he really believed in their truth, so far from offending, it was his duty to give the information, and instead of being punished, he should have been thanked by the Government. Not only was the honor of the flag involved, but the very safety of the Capitol. Porter saw that both were in danger by what he believed to be the incompetency of Pope. Was he to keep this conviction in his own breast, regardless of the army and the nation? Or was he not on the contrary, bound to speak his fears to those who had the power to guard against the apprehended peril? Were his fears honestly entertained? Was his motive for stating them patriotic? Let his dispatch to McClellan of first September, half-past eight P.M., give the answer. After telling him of Bayard's report of the movements of the enemy, he says: "I can see the dust and flags: columns evidently moving directly North: evidently towards Leesburgh. If you can, I hope you will protect the fords into Maryland, and guard the Railroad to Baltimore. I think we will have a fight before night. The enemy are between us and Fairfax Court-House, and shelled our trains last night. We will fight, or they will avoid us, and strike our rear first. We have been held on thirty-six hours too long, and we are bound to work our way to Alexandria. I only regret that we have not been distributed to forts, and to the fords over the Potomac into Maryland. GOD SPEED YOUR OPERATIONS, AND ENABLE YOU AND OTHERS IN AUTHORITY TO SAVE OUR COUNTRY," (p. 233.) His whole thoughts were evidently given to his country, its honor, and its safety. He apprehended, and as the result proved correctly, the marching of the enemy into Maryland, and perhaps further North. He was alarmed, too, (it was the alarm of a brave and patriotic man,) for the safety of the Capitol. He ardently wished to avert both dangers, and in words of patriotism that evidently gushed from his heart, he invoked McClellan to be on the alert—to watch the foe, and guard the passes, and prayed God to "speed" his "operation, and enable him," and "others in authority, to save the country." Alas! for our good name, this is the man who is charged with faithlessness to duty and treason to the nation. And as yet more dishonoring to it, this is the man whom a Court consisting of nine officers, have been induced to find guilty of the foul dishonoring crime, and whose sentence is supported by the highest military, legal officer, and in a moment of blindness to justice, the result of overconfidence in others, a sentence which the President, whose mind is naturally honest, to the prejudice of his own good name, without taking time properly to investigate the subject for himself, promptly approved. But is criticism on a commander's capacity, or of his plans by a subordinate officer so criminal as to demand, or at all justify dismissal from service? The wars of Europe furnish very many instances to the contrary. Even Napoleon, the strictest of disciplinarians as well as the greatest military man the world has ever known, not only did not punish, but encouraged it. He went further, he excused at times even a failure to obey orders. It is singular that this was not in the memory of the Judge-Advocate, affluent as it would seem to be with such learning.

When *Massena*, in 1810, was, against his wish, placed by Napoleon in command of the army of Portugal, and in spite of his criticisms to Napoleon himself on his plan of campaign, in obedience to orders, decided to lay siege to Ciudad Rodrigo, overruling in that respect the advice of his subordinates, Junot and Ney, who recommended an attack first upon that part of Wellington's army encamped at Viseu, Thiers tells us, that those two officers "spread abroad amongst their several corps, that it was *Massena, who, grown old*, and no longer the same man, preferred wearisome and murderous sieges to an active and "decisive campaign." (Vol. 12, *History of the Consulate and the Empire*, London edition, p. 151.) To criticise Napoleon, to advise against his plan of campaign, was harmless in Massena, and to disparage Massena with his army, was harmless in Junot and Ney. But for Porter to question Pope's plans, to speak despairingly of his strategy, though only to the superiors of both, to evince for Pope as a commander, though only to the superiors of both, "contemptuous and unfriendly feelings," is not to be tolerated or excused. Pope should have been held sacred, because infallible, and Porter condemned for questioning it—whilst Ney and Junot and Massena were properly esteemed guiltless, because Massena and Napoleon possessed no title to infallibility.

II. On the twelfth of March, 1811, after the triumph of the French in the battle of Redinha, Massena, who was still in command, implored Ney "to resist to the utmost, as the nature of the ground would well enable him to do, on his way to Condeixa." "Scarcely," says the same historian, "had Massena departed, than Ney began to watch the least movements of the English," and, hurried on by the fear of "being isolated from the main body" of the French army, "he disputed but for a few moments the heights of Condeixa, and then hastened to quit them." As soon as Massena heard of it he was indignant—"expressed aloud his indignation to Fririon, the chief of his staff, and was so greatly angered as to entertain for a moment the idea of depriving Ney of his command, and yet the purpose was only for a moment entertained, and, as far as we are informed, when he was acquainted with it, Napoleon never entertained it even for a moment, or thought that it required him even to censure Ney. Ney had, however, clearly violated a positive order, and by doing so, as the historian tells us, "for the sake of

avoiding an imaginary, or, at most, doubtful danger, he exposed the army to a certain peril," (ib. pp. 210, 211.) How striking is the contrast, even supposing an intended violation by Porter of the order of the twenty-seventh of August, between the conduct of Massena and Napoleon in Ney's case, and that of Pope, the Court, the Judge-Advocate, and the President, in Porter's case.

III. In November, 1812, when Wellington's whole army did not exceed sixty thousand men, and King Joseph's, Napoleon's brother, numbered eighty-five thousand, and Hill's command, left by Wellington at Alba de Tormes, fifteen thousand, the King, Jourdan and all the Generals but Soult, advised an "advance between the English Generals." Soult opposed it, and from deference to his authority the project which was apparently perfectly practicable, and might have led to the destruction of the English army, was abandoned, and another plan, advised by Soult, adopted. And then, on the thirteenth of the same month, when the French crossed the Tormes above Alba, and advanced as far as Neustra, Senora de Retiro, the King and Jourdan insisted upon the advisability of throwing the French cavalry upon the English army, visible on the right, Soult objected to the measure, on account of the obscurity of the atmosphere, etc." "and the result was, that when the eighty-five thousand French troops were assembled the English were already out of their reach, and in full retreat upon the Ciudad Rodrigo route," and the object of the campaign thereby lost, (ib. vol. 15, pp. 73, 74.) Soult nevertheless was continued in command, and escaped, as far as we know, even censure on the part of Napoleon. It can not be necessary to multiply instances from European armies. There are two recent ones, in our own army, occurring under the very eyes of the Government, that also strongly illustrate the injustice of the strict rule applied to Porter.

I. Whilst the Court-Martial in his case was in session, and in the same building, a military inquisition, instituted at the request of Major-General McDowell, of an extraordinary character was examining into the conduct of that officer, and with power to investigate his whole military career, although no charges of any kind had been made against him by any one in authority. Why this favor was shown to McDowell, and Porter was held to rigid and most technical proof, created in the minds of the observing, great surprise; but it is referred to in this connection with no view to censure. In the course of that inquisition, it appeared that McDowell had received a positive order from Pope, (under whose command he was,) which he failed to obey. Instead of doing so, he left his own troops and went in search of Pope, whose exact locality, however, he did not know. For this separation from his own corps, say the Court in his case, there was "clearly" nothing in another order upon which he relied, which contained even an implication to justify it. The result of his conduct, too, in that particular, had proved most disastrous, as proved by Pope, whose evidence in regard to it was adopted by the Court. Upon hearing of the battle, that a part of his corps had had that evening, Pope said : "I stated to several of my staff-officers who were present, that the game was in our own hands, (meaning, if his order had been executed,) that it was impossible for Jackson to escape without very heavy loss, if at all."

McDowell's excuse, that he desired to give "the expression of his views to General Pope in person," "could be of no avail when the misconduct of his own corps thwarted a plan, the execution of which afforded an opportunity for speedy victory."

To this unauthorized and inexcusable failure of McDowell, if it frustrated, as Pope says it did, the almost certain destruction of Jackson's command, and probably its capture, may with much more show of reason be attributed the failure of the campaign, (if that was not owing to the inherent defect of the plan of the campaign and the incompetency of the commander,) than to any or all of the failures, even were they established, alleged against Porter.

He, however, is cashiered, whilst McDowell is honorably acquitted, and at once placed on important duty, because, as the Court in his case say, gross as his fault was, "grave" as the "error committed by

him," (disobedience of an express order, which, as the Judge-Advocate says, and cites De Hart for it, "is a crime which the law has stigmatized as of the highest degree, and against which is denounced the extreme punishment of death,") "his subsequent efforts, on the twenty-ninth, to repair the consequences of that unfortunate movement of his corps, and to press them forward into action, were earnest and energetic, and disclosed fully that the separation of which this Court has stated its disapproval, was inconsiderate and unauthorized, but was *not induced by any unworthy motives.*" The italics are the Court's. And this moderate reproof, if reproof it can be called, is for the violation of a clear, positive order, leaving the subordinate no discretion, and committed upon his own judgment alone, without consulting, for aught that appeared, a single officer in his command.

His conduct "was not induced by any unworthy motive." Evidenced, in the Court's view, by his course on the following day. Had he confidence in Pope ? Was he asked ? If he had been, who that knows him, can doubt what his answer would have been, had he said what he thought ? The very fact, that at such a moment, he left his command in the hands of his own subordinates, to find Pope, to counsel with him as to the very order, and probably to advise against it, evinces strongly such want of confidence. But his next day's conduct exempts him from serious censure, as it proved his "motive" pure. And, besides, adds the Court, "it feels itself bound (why, but because it was material to the inquiry) to report the fact, that his commanding officer (General Pope) not only omitted to hold him culpable for this separation, but emphatically commended his whole conduct while under his command, without exception or qualification."

How different the facts and the course of the Court in Porter's case.

I. Before deciding not to attempt to execute the order of the twenty-seventh, by marching at one A.M., Porter was strongly advised against it by all of his general officers who were present when he received it. Officers, who have ever been above all suspicion of want of fidelity, and who now, and deservedly, stand high in Executive favor. On their almost positive remonstrance, he only agreed (they could persuade him to no longer delay) to wait till three A.M., but two hours, and he and they issued at once their orders accordingly; and who also proved that Bristow Station was reached as soon as if ·the march had been attempted at one.

II. His conduct on the bloody field of the thirtieth, red with the blood of thousands of his command, and illustrated by his usual fearless gallantry, and greatly diminishing the day's disaster.

III. Not only the omission of Pope even to intimate to him that he was held culpable for the alleged disobedience of the order of the twenty-seventh, but telling him, as he almost admits in his own evidence, and as was positively proved by Colonel Ruggles, (hereafter to be given,) that he had no fault to find; but, on the contrary, was satisfied with his whole conduct, and his omission afterward to report him to the Department, were all, in the judgment of the Court in his case, of no importance whatever, proving nothing in his favor, either as to act or intent—having not even a tendency to show that in his conduct in relation to the order, he "was not induced by any unworthy motive." For the one—McDowell—facts of the same character, not as strong, are a conclusive defense to proved disobedience. For the other—Porter—such facts, if they have any effect, either come "too late," or prove nothing, or if any thing, prove guilt. Such is the striking difference in the administration of its justice, exhibited by the Government through two of its Military Courts toward these two officers. The one, adjudged to be guiltless, and no doubt properly, who, from misfortune rather than want of skill, had signally failed *not only* to excite the admiration and gratitude of the Republic, but had received its censure—the other, adjudged guilty and cashiered, who, throughout his career, had evidenced rare skill and daring courage, and in the public estimation had won for himself a name of which the best of Napoleon's Marshals would have had reason to be proud.

How is this to be explained, and the reputation of the Government to pass unharmed? Can any reflecting, unprejudiced citizen give a satisfactory answer? And yet, how priceless to a "nation is even-handed justice." How imperative the interest, and the duty, to observe and enforce it.

But the opinion of the McDowell Court furnishes another instance of duty not performed in the same unfortunate campaign, and at the time known by Pope not to have been performed, and also by the War Department and the President, after that opinion was given—and yet, to this day, not even censured. And what makes that instance the more striking, is, that it was on the part of General King, one of the members of the Court that convicted and sentenced Porter. The division of that officer, as Pope testified before the McDowell Court, had had a successful fight with the enemy, "who were retreating from Centreville, on the night of the twenty-eighth of August, had remained masters of the field, still interposing between Jackson's forces and the main body of the enemy, and that the information was, he thought, brought to him by a staff-officer of General King." This filled him, as it well might, with high hopes of success, and he says that he "immediately" "directed General Kearny, whose division occupied Centreville, to push forward cautiously at one o'clock that night, in the direction of Gainesville, to drive in the pickets of the enemy," etc. "I directed him, at the first blush of daylight, to attack the enemy with his right advanced, and informed him that Hooker and Reno would be with him immediately after daylight. *To my surprise and dissatisfaction,* I learned toward daylight, on the morning of the twenty-ninth, that King's division had been withdrawn in the direction of Manassas Junction, leaving open the road to Thoroughfare Gap. This withdrawal of that division made necessary a great change in the movement, *and was a most serious and unlooked for mistake.*" McDowell, under whose command King was, had before left his corps improperly, as the Court found. He, of course, did not give King the order to withdraw. If he had, the Court says, "it could not be controverted that he would be justly held responsible for their retreat. and the consequent derangements of the plan of battle then formed by General Pope." By whose order, then, was the retreat made? By King's. Why was not he called to answer for it? Did he know that it was important to hold his ground? Pope says that he was "so impressed with the necessity, that that division (King's) should hold its ground, that I sent several orders to General King (*one by his own staff-officer,*) during that night, to hold his ground at all hazards, and to prevent the retreat of the enemy, and informed him that our whole force from the direction of Centreville and Manassas Junction would fall upon the enemy at daylight."

The testimony of General Pope, in relation to these orders, the Court adopt, "as a faithful statement of the facts." Was the first order, or either of the succeeding ones, known to or received by King? If they were, how is 'it that he has not been charged with disobedience? If he did know of the orders, did he satisfy his before *surprised and dissatisfied chief* that he had good grounds for his disobedience, or, at least, that he "was not induced by any unworthy motive," or has he since satisfied the Department? If he has, then disobedience is not always censurable. Then "the Napoleonic maxim" includes ends as well as means.

That General King, who is known to be a patriotic soldier, had good motives for his failure, disastrous as Pope says it was to his plans, those who are acquainted with him will readily believe.

But to condemn Porter of disobedience, and to cashier him in the face of the reasons which are proved to have governed him, the concurrent and strong advice, and almost remonstrance, of his three Generals, and when the order itself afterward proved to be useless, and not only not to question King, but, on the contrary, to make him one of Porter's judges, and to continue him in high command, is conduct on the part of those in authority which no explanation can justify or excuse.

III. A yet more recent case, in the Army of the Potomac, illustrates still stronger the injustice done to Porter. On the removal from its command, as we all unfortunately now know it to have been, of General McClellan, General Burnside was placed at its head. The high character for gallantry and patriotism of that soldier no one that has watched his career will ever question. Whether it was well or ill advised, his subsequent attack on the enemy at Fredericksburgh, proved most disastrous. To redeem the honor of his army, and retrieve, at the same time, his own weakened reputation, he resolved on an other attack, and on a different plan. This was at once, not to him only, but to all, criticised with severity by his officers; and two of his Generals, with, as it was stated, the knowledge of others, visited the President to protest against it, and did so. The result was, the President, on their advice, prohibited the movement. Burnside at once, before he had seen the President, for this insubordination, issued an order, subject to the President's approval, dismissing from the service several of the highest officers in his command, and many others, and, soon after, informed the President in person that his sanctioning the order was indispensable not only to his remaining in command of the army, but to his continuing in the military service. He testified, as the reader will remember, before the Committee of Congress on the Conduct of the War, that the President told him that his order of dismissal was right, but that before acting upon it, he must consult his advisers, and that by persuasion he induced the witness to relinquish his purpose to leave the service. The result, and as it is to be supposed of his consultation with his Cabinet, was that not only were none of the officers who were to be dismissed by the order dismissed, but, on the contrary, that General Hooker, one of the number, was put in the chief command.

Here again criticisms showing, if unexplained, "contempt" for the skill of a Commander-in-Chief may be so explained as to be held innocent, and may even place, notwithstanding his own example of insubordination, one of the critics in the place of the Chief.

IV. Another strong instance must be in the recollection of all. General Charles P. Stone, more than a year since, for alleged disloyalty and insinuated charge of treason, was taken from his then command, and for many weary months imprisoned in Fort Lafayette. Futile were his and his friends' efforts to ascertain what were the specific acts of disloyalty, or the grounds of imputed treason. No explanation was given or could be obtained. And when his case was made a matter of inquiry in the Senate of the United States, the Chairman of the Military Committee of that body, who was also Chairman of the Committee on the Conduct of the War, stated, in substance, that the evidence before the latter committee fully justified the imprisonment, and the President afterward, in replying to a call of the Senate, virtually said the same thing. But now what a change. No Court-Martial or inquiry was ordered, though frequently solicited by Stone. No specification or other definition of the charges ever given him, and yet but the other day he was ordered into service in the Army of the Gulf, and is now at the head of the command which recently so distinguished itself under the lead of the gallant Sherman. Porter's case then, though of the same character of those named, is the only one which, in the opinion of the authorities, it has been deemed necessary to inquire into, much less to punish. He is the only officer who, upon such grounds, has been held unfit for a service which he has so adorned, and not to be relied upon to aid the country, which, during the present war, he has so signally served and so fondly loves.

But to return to the evidence, it is said by the Judge-Advocate, that neither the character of the night, nor the state of the road, nor the condition of his command excused Porter for his failure literally to comply with the order to start at one A.M. These objections will be considered in their order.

I.—As to the Night.

Its darkness had been given as a reason for not starting at one A.M. The Judge-Advocate answers this as he does every part of the case by giving but detached and partial statements of the evidence of a few of the witnesses, and omitting altogether what was proved by those who were clearly the most to be relied upon. The parts of the testimony that he does give, are from the evidence of Captain Duryea, Major Barstow, Lieutenant-Colonel Myers, General Pope, and General

Roberts. What was proved by Generals Morell, Griffin, Sykes, Butterfield and Reynolds, Colonel Cleary, Lieutenant-Colonel Locke, Captain Fifield, and Montieth, and Lieutenant Weld, all present when the order was received, or was being executed, is not given at all, and the reader will ask why? And can he give a satisfactory answer? This obviously unfair omission will now be supplied.

1. *Morell* says: "It was a *very* dark night. It was cloudy, threatening to rain, and did rain before morning." (P. 145.)

2. *Griffin.*—"The night of the twenty-seventh, and the morning of the twenty-eighth *was very* dark," I "know that at three o'clock, it was very dark, so dark that I used candles with my leading regiments to get through a little piece of woods which we left, in which we had been encamped." (Pp. 160–63.)

3. *Sykes.*—"The night was unusually dark." "Before I directed the advance to be sounded, I sent an aid-de-camp to find the road, so as to lead the column upon it. He returned in a short time, and told me that the darkness was so great, that he could not distinguish the road. He also told me that he was assisted in that search by several soldiers." (Pp. 176, 177.)

4. *Butterfield*, after stating, as before mentioned, what occurred in Porter's tent, when the order was received, and Porter's answer to the objections of his Generals to his marching at one A.M., added: "When we got outside, the darkness was so apparent, (to use such an expression,) and it seemed such a matter of impossibility to move, that General Porter said: "In consideration of all the circumstances, I will fix the hour at three o'clock instead of one. You will be ready to move promptly." He also stated that De Kay, who was sent by Pope with the order, said: "That it would be very difficult in getting back. That he would have hard work to find the way." (Pp. 185, 186.)

5. *Reynolds*, (alas! now of our illustrious dead.)—"It was a *very dark night*, as was the succeeding night. I recollect both of

them *distinctly from having been about a good deal, until after twelve o'clock on each night."* (P. 169.)

6. *Cleary.* — "It was dark, cloudy." (P. 121.)

7. *Locke.* — The night was *"extremely dark." "I received a very severe injury, groping about in the darkness."* (P. 134.)

8. *Fifield.* — "The early part of the night was an ordinary star-light night of summer, without any moon. About half-past eleven o'clock, it commenced overcasting, and threatened rain. Very black clouds came up, and it did sprinkle a little. *It was very dark from that time till toward morning."*
"It was very dark," "every thing so obscure from the *extreme darkness* of the night, that it would be very difficult for me to give any thing like a reasonable answer, in regard to that matter." (The matter was as to the extent and density of the wood along the road.) He also said "the night was very dark, and it was like a man groping his way in the darkness, without being able to see his hand before him, much of the way through the wood." (Pp. 122–125.)
This witness testified also that he was on duty from half-past ten o'clock, the entire balance of the night.

9. *Montieth.* — The night was *"very dark."* (P. 126.)

10. *Weld.* — The night *"was very dark indeed."* (P. 129.)

With all this evidence before him, the Judge-Advocate advises the President, that the night was not so dark before eleven o'clock, at least, if at any hour, as to have made it impossible for Porter, "to obey the order," to move at one A.M., and that it was a noticeable fact, "that the determination not to move at that hour, was not occasioned by *this* extreme darkness, (the admission that the darkness was extreme, thus leaked out,) but had been taken before Captain De Kay lay down, which was at eleven o'clock." And this is told to the President, though the Judge-Advocate knew, or should have known,

that General Butterfield had before testified *positively*, that Porter, and that, too, unwillingly, only agreed to postpone the time of marching from one to three A.M., when he, with his Generals, got outside of his tent and saw "the darkness so apparent," that it "seemed to be such a matter of impossibility to move." It was then, and not before that Porter yielded to the advice and remonstrance of his three Generals, saying : "In consideration of all the circumstances I will fix the hour at three o'clock, instead of one." Why was the fact represented otherwise, and without even an intimation, that there was proof to the contrary? And especially, why was the President not informed of this evidence of Butterfield? It can not be necessary to say more on this head.

II.—THE CONDITION OF THE ROAD.

That, says the Judge-Advocate, afforded no excuse for failing to march at one A.M. However dark the night was—whatever may have been the condition of his men—however worn down by immediately preceding day and night marches—however deprived of rest and food, there was nothing in the condition of the roads, that offered even an apology for not moving. But to the fact. What was the condition of the road?
The witnesses who were on the road that night, Major Cleary and Captain Fifield proved beyond all cavil, the existence of serious obstructions.

1. *Cleary.*—"At ten o'clock that night, I received a note from General Porter to move the trains east of the railroad beyond, and east of Cedar Run, toward Bristow Station. I gave the order to the proper persons connected with the trains, and they commenced immediately to move," "the removal of the trains occupied me from ten o'clock, till two o'clock in the morning, at which time, or perhaps a little later, I myself left that point for Bristow Station." "The road for some three miles, I think, was occupied by wagons, and was obstructed so as to render it very difficult for me and my party to pass along." (P. 121.) He testified also that his party consisted of ten or twelve persons only, that he traveled on horseback, and that they did not get to Bristow Station that night.

2. *Fifield*—He testified that he received through Colonel Cleary, an order from General Porter on the evening of the twenty-seventh of August, "to have the trains moved from Warrenton Junction down as far as possible in the neighborhood of Bristow Station." He said that he proceeded to execute it, and that it was not fully effected till about four o'clock in the morning, because it could not have been sooner done, and added, "that the moving of the trains during the night, would have prevented the possibility of moving troops on the railroad track." He also said, that between "three and four miles" of the road, (not the railroad,) was occupied by wagons, and in reply to inquiries of the Judge-Advocate, stated: "I know of no road except on one side, (that is, on one side of the railroad,) and that the wagons on that, were very much jammed and remaining stationary. I found a great deal of difficulty even in getting through them on horseback." (Pp. 122–124.)

III.—THE CONDITION OF THE TROOPS.

1. *Morell.* — They were *very much exhausted from their previous marching.* They had marched all the way from James River, except from Fortress Monroe to Acquia Creek." "They had marched (laboriously) and as fast as possible," "and sometimes at night." On being told by Porter of the order, he said, that he, and *Sykes* and *Butterfield*, "immediately spoke of the condition of our troops, *they being so much fatigued*," as well as of "the darkness of the night, and told him that we did not believe we could make any better progress by attempting to start at that hour, (one A.M.) than if we waited till daylight." (Pp. 144, 145.)

2. *Sykes.*—I told Porter, on his informing me of the order to march at one A.M., my reasons for his not attempting it, "That a night march is always exceedingly fatiguing and injurious to troops. *That my command had already marched from twelve to fourteen miles that day,*" etc. (P. 176.)

3. *Butterfield.* — My men "*were very much fatigued.* They had marched from Kelly's Ford to Bealton, and from there up to Warrenton Junction, almost all the way without water, in the dust. It was very warm, and it was with great difficulty that we got them along." (P. 186.)

No portion of this testimony was the President advised of, and yet its materiality is most apparent. Why did the Judge-Advocate omit it, in executing an order, which directed him to report "*fully*" upon the bearing of all the testimony? Why select a part? Can these inquiries possibly be met satisfactorily? What fair mind will say they can?

The darkness of the night then, the state of the road, the condition of the troops, rendered it, in the opinion of his three Generals, not only inadvisable, but *impossible*, to execute literally as to time, the order of the twenty-seventh of August. Did the President, when he approved the sentence, know these facts? For the sake of his own character, of his sense of justice, his duty to the country, it is hoped, and believed, that he did not. Did he know, could he have known, that Porter's decision was based not on his own experience merely, but, as proved by *Sykes*, "upon the opinions of the three General officers in his corps next in rank to himself," (p. 176,) and that each one of them, in his testimony before the Court, maintained the same opinion?

Did he know, that all concurred in saying that "nothing whatever" would have been gained by a different decision? And, finally, did he know, what they all also stated, (as did Pope,) that the "military necessity for the movement to be at one o'clock A.M., on the twenty-eighth, so as to be at Bristow Station at daylight, did not appear, on the twenty-eighth," when Porter's command reached that point? (P. 177.)

Ignorance, however, of these circumstances can not be used in vindication of the Court. How they are to be vindicated, except upon the hypothesis of an obtuseness of intellect, the effect of prejudice, no fair mind can imagine.

But in the march, when it was begun, the Judge-Advocate says, "there was no haste or vigor displayed," and that the mud, spoken of by General *Griffin*, could not have been an obstacle "at such a season." "It was (he adds) in summer, and a season of drought, as appears from the clouds of dust which are continually brought to our notice by the testimony," and that "he can not, therefore, be misled," by the alleged existence of mud.

A few words on these points are all that can be necessary :

1. The charge of the absence of haste and vigor rests on the evidence of De Kay. On his statement that the troops were marched "at the rate at which troops would move if there was no necessity for rapid movement," and that, in his "judgment," they could "have moved much faster than they did in point of fact."

In the first place, the evidence of this witness, who was on Pope's staff, is to be taken with many grains of allowance. He recollects little except what was thought to prejudice Porter. He remembers nothing of what Porter said to the attending Generals, except that he states Porter said, "Gentlemen, there is something for you to sleep upon," a fact positively disproved by Butterfield, and not stated by Sykes or Morell.

2. He said, "he could not recollect *precisely*" whether Porter announced his purpose, either to obey the order or not, a fact clearly proved by each of the Generals.

3. That he " was aware of the determination not to start until *daylight*," because *he* " went to sleep" on hearing so, when the Generals, all of them say, at first he resolved starting at once, and only delayed till three through their earnest advice.

4. He does not say, what Butterfield proved he did say, that he told Porter " it would be very difficult in getting back. That he would have hard work to find the way."

But, it is not necessary to rely on these circumstances. As the fact of the asserted want of haste and vigor, is *positively disproved* by each of the Generals, and by other officers, a fact also not disclosed to the President.

1. *Morell* answered "*Yes*" to this question : " After starting at three o'clock, did your own command, and so far as you know, the rest of the corps make the *best*

of their way, and push on as fast as possible toward Bristow Station ?" (P. 145.)

2. *Sykes.*—"I led the advance on that morning, (the twenty-eighth,) and I continued my march to Bristow Station, with the exception of the usual halts which commands always have to allow men to pass to the rear, and the one that I spoke of at the creek, when I said, I found it necessary to halt my command for some time, in order to unite it." (P. 179.)

3. *Locke.*—"They (the troops) marched as fast as they could under the circumstances," and by the circumstances, he said, he meant " the darkness of the night, and the obstructions of the road." He also stated that the troops " were very much fatigued." (P. 134.)

How idle to disregard all this concurring proof, and rely not only on the unsupported but the contradicted evidence of *De Kay*. And how unfair to the President and to the public, (the review was intended for both,) and unjust to Porter, not to give the opposing and contradictory evidence.

II. That the mud was no obstacle " to the onward march of soldiers determined to do their duty." No evidence was offered to prove that there was no mud on any part of the line of march.

I. The Judge-Advocate infers it " from the clouds of dust " continually brought to our notice by the evidence. How illogical. What rare simplicity. The weather was hot and dry. The parts of the road where there was no water, were dusty. There could not, therefore, be mud, where there was no dust, but water. Had the exigency of his case required it, the acute and learned reviewer would have maintained, that as Pennsylvania Avenue is at times excruciatingly dusty, there can not then be mud in the marshes of the Potomac.

II. But the fact of there being mud, and that it operated to impede the march, was proved expressly by Generals Griffin and Butterfield. They were on the spot, leading the march of their respective columns, and it is rather more than probable, that they would know better whether there was mud in the route, and whether it interposed an obstacle to the march, than an official sitting in his study, and evidently bent on showing that there was nothing in the way to impede "the onward march of soldiers determined to do their duty."

1. *Griffin.*—"I know that the artillery which followed the brigade, that is, a carriage or two of the artillery which followed the brigade, got *stuck in the mud*, or in a little creek, and had trouble in getting out. (P. 161.)

2. *Butterfield.*—In answer to a question by the Judge-Advocate, he said: "I know that after it had got to be about daylight, I went out to the head of my column, and I found a difficult place to cross—that there was difficulty in getting the troops across. I could see that it had been dark, and the troops had been impeded, but they began to go on more rapidly, as light broke."

He was then asked again by the Judge-Advocate to "state the character of the difficulty—the character of the place—was it mud or water, or what was it?" And he answered:

"It was *mud and water both*—one of those streams that we almost always have to *force troops over*. In the daytime you could force them over very well—but at night, when it can not be seen, it is a *very difficult thing* to get men across such a place." (P. 187.)

This testimony of Butterfield is not even alluded to in the review. Then, unless Griffin and Butterfield swear falsely, (for mistake as to such facts was impossible,) notwithstanding the hypothesis of the Judge-Advocate, resting on the existence of dust on portions of the road, there was mud and water in other portions, and to an extent interposing obstacles "to the onward march of soldiers determined to do their duty." But, finally, on this head. Why is it, that Porter, alone of the command is accused of want of "haste or vigor"?

As commander of the entire corps, his duty was but to issue the necessary orders to his division commanders, for the march. And this they all say, was done. It was their duty to superintend the execution of the orders. They are equally responsible for disregard of duty, as their immediate chief. He relied, as he had a right to rely, upon them to conduct the march with proper "haste" and "vigor." He had every reason for such reliance. They had been under his command on many battlefields. He had seen them in the midst of countless perils, ever foremost in danger, unsurpassed in skill, and nobly devoted to duty. "To do their duty," he knew them to be "soldiers determined." If there was any failure, then, in the speed of the march, it is to be referred to them, and not to him." And yet, who has ever called their patriotism, or their efforts in regard to it, in question? The Government certainly has not. They are now, and have been continuously, from the twenty-seventh of August, eighteen hundred and sixty-two, in its service, and on duty. To hold Porter responsible for their alleged misconduct, (for which, however, there is not the least ground,) and not only not even to censure them, but to keep them in honored commands, is an unequal measure of justice, that amounts to a gross and palpable wrong. One victim, however, was enough. To have sacrificed to the behest of ⬤rty, or to the exigencies of an ill-planned campaign, and of an unfortunately selected Commander, Morell, Griffin and Butterfield, would have been too glaringly to have outraged public opinion, and it was not done. But the very omission of passing by these officers, and visiting upon their immediate chief, the sole responsibility for the asserted want of haste and vigor in the march of the twenty-eighth of August, which, if it was true, was their fault, and not his, demonstrates the depth and the enormity of the injustice done to Porter.

SECOND SPECIFICATION—FIRST CHARGE.

II. The second specification of the first charge is, Porter's failure to obey the joint order to himself and McDowell of the twenty-ninth August, eighteen hundred and sixty-two. That order was as follows:

"HEADQUARTERS ARMY OF VIRGINIA,
CENTREVILLE, August 29th, 1862.
"GENERALS McDOWELL AND PORTER:
"You will please move forward with your joint command towards Gainesville.

I sent General Porter written orders to that effect, an hour and a half ago. Heintzelman, Sigel, and Reno, are moving on the Warrenton turnpike, and must now be not far from Gainesville. I desire that as soon as communication is established between this force and your own, the whole command shall halt. It may be necessary to fall back behind Bull Run to-night. I presume it will be so on account of our supplies.

"I have sent no orders of any description to Ricketts, and none to interfere in any way with the movement of General McDowell's troops, except what I sent by his aid-de-camp last night, which were to hold his position on the Warrenton pike, until the troops from here should fall on the enemy's flank and rear.

"I do not even know Ricketts's position, as I have not been able to find out where General McDowell was until a late hour this morning.

"General McDowell will take immediate steps to communicate with General Ricketts, and instruct him to join the other division of his corps as soon as practicable. If any considerable advantages are to be gained by departing from this order, it will not be strictly ⬤ried out. One thing must be held in view, that the troops must occupy a position, from which they can reach Bull Run to-night, or by morning. The indications are, that the whole force of the enemy is moving in this direction, at a pace that will bring them here by to-morrow night, or the next day. My own headquarters will for the present be with Heintzelman's or at this place.

"JOHN POPE,
"Major-General Commanding."

I. The first inquiry on this head is, what, in one particular, was the meaning of the order? Was it that each of the two Generals was to act independently of each other, or that, being together when received, and being executed, they were to be governed by the sixty-second Article of War? This, as will be seen, is a material point, and was so considered by the Judge-Advocate. He endeavors to give it the former interpretation, and relies for that purpose mainly on Pope's evidence. Pope, he says, testified that his "intention" was, that they "should

act independently of each other, and each in direct subordination to himself." (P. 306.) But even with this assistance, he admits that the point is not clear. Anxious as he was to maintain that construction, he could not bring himself to say, in its support, more than that "under these circumstances, it may *well be questioned*" whether, under the Article of War referred to "General McDowell could continue the command which he had assumed over these joint forces." Here, again, as throughout, contrary to the universal rule, doubt, however reasonable, is to be solved to the prejudice of Porter. "Full weight," says Bennet, and all other authorities, is to be given "to every argument or presumption in favor of the prisoner." (P. 126.) Porter was, by the Court and Judge-Advocate, denied the benefit of this rule.

In fact, however, there is no room for doubt. The construction maintained by the Judge-Advocate as probable, is manifestly wrong.

II. To call to the aid of that construction Pope's oral proof before the Court, of his intention, is in violation of the best-established rules of evidence.

The order must be its own interpreter. To construe written matter by evidence *aliunde*, every professional man knows to be inadmissible. Nothing but confusion, mistake and injustice would be the result of such a course. And in this instance, to refer to Pope's evidence, given months after the order, not made known to McDowell and Porter when they received it, or afterward, until he gave such evidence, is as absurd as it is unjust. How were either of them to know Pope's intention, except as the order disclosed it? He was twelve miles away from them. The order was received, without any explanation or message from Pope. His mind, his intent, they could but collect from the order itself; and certainly they could not foresee that, months afterward, Pope would seek to give it an intent, not only not consentaneous with, but contradictory with its terms. Pope is presumed to have known of the sixty-second Article of War. If by that article, McDowell, as "the officer highest in rank," would have the right to "command the whole," then, at least, in the absence of any direction from himself to the contrary, Pope is to be assumed to have so intended.

The different view taken by the Judge-Advocate serves to deprive Porter of the defense to this specification, that in what he is charged to have done, or to have omitted, in supposed violation of this order, he acted under the command of General McDowell, his senior in rank.

The very fact that such a view is taken by the Judge-Advocate, satisfactorily shows, that he thought the opposite one would, upon the evidence, be a full answer to the specification. He seeks also to maintain his interpretation upon the further ground, that the article "excludes the idea of the presence of an officer superior in rank to those commanding the different corps of which it speaks." Certainly it does. But was Pope present when he gave the order? when it was received? or was being executed? The Judge-Advocate does not say he was, but does say he "was absent but a few miles." How many miles, he does not inform the President, or how many miles would, in his opinion, constitute absence and not presence. As the fact in this connection was material, he should have stated if he knew, and he ought to have known, the evidence being before him, how far off Pope was, that the President might judge, as he gave no opinion of his own to guide him, whether such distance was absence or not. Pope was at *Centreville*, a distance of *twelve miles*. To say then that he was present would seem to be absurd. The Article looks to present and immediate joint duty.

It was such duty that the order embraced. The two commands were to act together. The officers were told to "move forward with your *joint command* toward Gainesville." It contemplated its union with the forces of *Heintzelman*, *Sigel*, and *Reno*, and that that occurring, "the whole force should halt." They were also told, "that the troops (that is, all of them) must occupy a position from which they can reach Bull Run to-night or by morning." In the forward movement of the two corps, who was to command? Who to give the order to halt? Who to de-

cide upon the position to be held to enable the command to reach Bull Run that night or morning?

The Article contemplates this very state of things, and provides for it. "If on marches," or "doing duty together" different corps of the army shall happen to join, the officer highest in rank of the line of the army, "shall command the whole, and give orders for what is needful to the service." No matter how the junction is brought about, when it exists, the Article embraces it, and establishes a positive rule, that "the officer highest in rank in the line of the army" is to command the whole with the single exception that it shall be "otherwise specially directed by the President of the United States." To hold that, under the circumstances of this joint command, what was to be done in executing the joint order, was to be done by Pope, who was *twelve miles distant*, upon the theory that he was, notwithstanding, to be considered present, every one will see is wholly untenable. How was he to judge when to move the command? when to halt, or what position to take with a view to retire to Bull Run that night or the next morning? These two corps were placed by the order and the sixty-second Article under the command of McDowell. No one but the President had the authority to take the command out of the operation of that Article. And even if Pope thought that he had the power, he did not attempt to exert it by the joint order.

II. The specification does not state in what particular the order was disobeyed. It only alleges that Porter "did then and there disobey."

We are to look then, to the evidence and review, for the information. The finding of the Court, merely finds disobedience in fact, without stating in what it consisted.

The President therefore had no knowledge upon the point, except as he obtained it from the Review. That told him that, "the Court concluded and justly, that his (Porter's) falling back under the circumstances, and for the purpose mentioned in his note to Generals McDowell and King, was a violation of the joint order to himself and McDowell." (P. 308.)

As this is the only information we have of what was considered by the Court disobedience, it would be sufficient to confine these remarks to that point. But, as the Judge-Advocate has suggested many things, tending to disparage Porter in other particulars, these will be first noticed.

I. It is said, that when the two corps were together, and the front of Porter's column (his corps being in advance) "had reached some three miles beyond *Bethlehem Church*," "General McDowell then rode forward to the head of the column of the accused, when an interview and conference took place between them. They discussed the joint order, and General McDowell determined, *for himself*, that there were considerable advantages to be gained by departing from it," and by moving with his forces along the Sudley Springs road toward the field of a battle, then being fought by the main army of General Pope, at the distance of three or four miles. His purpose was to throw himself on the enemy's centre, and he wished the accused to attack his right flank. He then said to Porter: "You put your forces in here, and I will take mine up the Sudley Springs road on the left of troops engaged at that point with the enemy." (P. 307.)

From this statement, the reader will suppose that McDowell considered himself entitled to direct Porter's movement. The Judge-Advocate should at least be consistent with himself. If upon the theory that Pope was to be considered as present, Porter was not under McDowell's command, then the latter had no right to direct his movements. Of these Porter had the sole control, subject only to Pope.

If they were to "act independently of each other," (and the Judge-Advocate says they were to do so,) and that such was Pope's "intention," then if McDowell's alleged direction to Porter was given authoritatively, it was but intrusive. If on the contrary, as in this part of his review, the Judge-Advocate implies, a different opinion of their relation toward each other, is the correct one, Porter was under the command of McDowell, then it is most important to ascertain what order, if any, was given by the latter to Porter. If he was subject to McDowell's command, (as it is confidently believed, and as in this part of his argument, is conceded by the Judge-Advocate,) then his duty in the execution of the joint order was to act in subordination to that officer. And if in doing so, the joint order was disobeyed, the offender was McDowell, not Porter. Where was McDowell, when he gave the order to Porter, and what was that order?

I. He was present with the joint command, and had the control of it. His leaving it afterward, and going with his own corps to another part of the field, in no way impairs the validity or effect of his prior order; whatever that was, Porter was bound to obey it.

II. If McDowell gave an order, what was it?

The Judge-Advocate would have us believe, that it was that Porter should attack "the enemy's right flank"—should put his "force in here," meaning, in front of the then locality of the two corps. He does not intimate even, that a word was uttered by McDowell contrary to this alleged order, and yet the proof is clear, (McDowell to the contrary, notwithstanding,) that there was an order, and not only that, but that the one alleged was not given at all.

I. *Lieutenant-Colonel Locke*, Chief of Porter's staff, and his Assistant Adjutant-General. He saw McDowell on the twenty-ninth, "on the ground where he had taken up our position in the direction of Gainesville," and near the Manassas Railroad," "where Porter was forming his corps in line of battle." "He had made considerable progress in the disposition of his troops, a battery was in position, and the troops were being deployed. Skirmishers were being thrown out in front." On seeing it, McDowell said: "Porter, you are out too far already, this is no place to fight a battle." (P. 135.)

If this evidence is to be relied upon, (and this will soon be examined,) Porter was preparing for battle. He was not then certainly providing for "the personal safety of (himself) and staff," as the reviewer most charitably suggests, was his motive subsequently in another asserted movement on the same day.

2. *Captain A. P. Martin,* a Captain in the Third Massachusetts battery, commanding "Division Artillery of General Morell's division." He saw a meeting between McDowell and Porter, about eleven o'clock on the morning of the twenty-ninth, "on the road leading from Manassas Junction to Gainesville," and "at the head of the column," (Porter's.) Heard McDowell say to Porter: "PORTER, THIS IS NO PLACE TO FIGHT A BATTLE, YOU ARE OUT TOO FAR." Colonel Locke, he said was present, and within hearing at the time. Porter "had sent out skirmishers to the front, and the troops were moving, closing up apparently *en masse,* as I supposed, preparing to form a line of battle, *which was afterward done.* These movements "were continued. The brigade that was leading were being disposed off, on the hill near where the conversation referred to, had taken place—one brigade, and one battery moved off to the right shortly after, evidently preparing to form on the right of the brigade on the hill. I went with the battery that moved to the right, to see the position. One battery was placed where the conversation was held, about that time." (P. 144.)

Both of these witnesses were unimpeached by evidence as to character or otherwise, and in their cross-examination, the Judge-Advocate made no attempt to weaken their testimony. Not a question was propounded, suggesting even a possibility that they could be mistaken. And when McDowell was recalled for the purpose, in part, of rebutting this evidence, he was only asked by the Judge-Advocate, if he had or not, "recollection of having said to Porter," at his interview with him on the twenty-ninth, (he had admitted the fact of the interview,) what was sworn to by Locke and Martin, and his answer was: "I can not recollect *precisely* what occurred, or *what conversation,* and what words passed between us at that time. I can not say what language I used, or how it may have been understood, whilst talking on that point," (the joint order.) (Pp. 217, 218.)

He stated also, that he thought the conversation related chiefly to Pope's joint order. It is then, but a failure to remember whether he did or not tell Porter what Locke and Martin positively testified. *Non me recordo.* In using this phrase, a classic one, since the trial of England's former Queen, it is not intended 'to intimate, that it was the purpose of McDowell to conceal what he did know, but merely to show that his evidence rebutted nothing, but merely proved a want of memory, as to the fact that he was called to rebut. Every lawyer, every man of sense, knows, that such evidence has not a feather's weight against positive proof. Intelligent experience ever discards it as wholly unreliable. If, in this instance, influence was given to it, it is but another proof of the weakness to which prejudice has reduced the minds of the Court.

The state of things then existing at eleven A.M., on the twenty-ninth, was:

I. That Porter was preparing for battle at the point where McDowell and he met. That his corps were all placed by his order, or were being placed in position for that purpose.

II. That he was told by McDowell, that he was not to fight there, the place not being a proper one for a battle, and that "he was too far advanced." McDowell supposed he was too far forward, that his position was an unfit one, and, of course, a dangerous one, for a conflict, and yet it is insinuated by the Judge-Advocate, that he retreated an hour or two only afterward, on the same day, for the degrading and cowardly purpose of securing "the personal safety of (himself) and staff." (P. 308.)

Was ever a party dealt with so unjustly? Could it have been thought possible, that a gallant officer, who in the many battles through which he had passed, was always in the front, or where danger was greatest—devoting his energies, and periling his life for the honor and existence of his country, whilst the Judge-Advocate was safely seated in his office, where no danger could come, or if it did, could readily be escaped from, would be arraigned by that officer, before the President and the public, as having abandoned his duty, and cravenly fled from the foe for the vile and disgraceful purpose of "personal safety." Is all generosity gone? Is no magnanimity left? Is all gratitude fled? It is of the many dreadful evils of this war, that suspicion takes the place of confidence, prejudice of impartiality, the darkest passions of the highest virtues. Porter a coward! Let him who charges it, go to the noble troops he has so often led to battle, and ask of them if the charge is not true. He would soon be found, if not himself wholly regardless of danger, looking to his "personal safety." Go to the officers who have been with him in battle, and never saw his eye dimmed, except when he discovered his comrades wounded and dying around him, and see with what surprise and scorn the charge would be received. Go to the troops and the officers constituting his corps on the twenty-ninth, and listen to the contempt with which the imputation would be regarded. The enlightened public will never sanction such an accusation by whomsoever made. They are ever grateful to such a public servant as they know Porter to have been. Individuals may be found wanting in that virtue. But such a public, never. Ingratitude, that "crime of deeper die than all the guilty train of human vices," is never found in them.

III. Conceding, however, that the joint order did not direct an attack on the enemy at that point, or elsewhere, on that day, and that McDowell gave Porter no such order, or if he did, that it was without authority, the Judge-Advocate says: "It would *seem* to have been a manifest violation of the duty resting on Porter in the position in which he was then placed, without reference to any specific order or direction, leading or directing him to engage the enemy," not to have done so. (P. 308.)

I. It would be a conclusive reply to this view that the specification charges only disobedience of the joint order of the twenty-ninth. If it was the purpose of the Judge-Advocate to rely on any such general military duty, as is here stated, fairness, as well as the laws of military

pleading, required that it should have been alleged. To specify a particular offense, and on the trial rely upon another and totally different one, is as repugnant to justice as to every legal principle. How is the accused to prepare for his defense? to know what witnesses to summon? or what proof he is to meet? It is impossible that the law in this respect can be unknown to the Judge-Advocate. A long abandonment of the profession, which he for years so greatly adorned, may have had its usual result, the making him somewhat rusty in some branches of the science. But this rule of pleading and evidence is so familiar, and so challenges the assent of every sensible mind, that he could not have forgotten it. Why then rely on a charge not stated in the specification? Why present it to the President as one of the reasons for his approving the finding on the actual specification? Can it be accounted for except because he was satisfied, or apprehended the President would be satisfied that the offense specified was not established by the evidence? Did he urge the same view upon the Court? Did the Court adopt it, or itself take it? If so, both he and the Court offended against the law, and committed a legal outrage upon Porter. The same observations are applicable to the further view of the Judge-Advocate, that Porter on the same day violated an "elementary principle," "that in the absence of positive restraining orders, the march shall always be toward the sound of the guns. (Ib.) That is not the offense specified. Nothing can be clearer than this. But, waiving this objection, conclusive as it is, what foundation in fact is there for either of these charges?

II. The ground of the first is said to be, that the officer is bound to hold his column so, "in the advance, as to be ready to afford mutual assistance in time of need." (Ib.) *Need*, then, is to exist, to make the principle applicable. Who is to judge of it? The officer in command of the column. If he judges erroneously, it is no offense, provided he does so honestly. Those who know Porter require no proof to convince them that, unless prohibited by "restraining orders," he would ever assist his brother soldiers in time of need. Did he believe it was wanted in this instance? The columns supposed to have required his aid were not in his sight, but several miles off. Nor could he leave his own command to ascertain their condition, or the desire of their immediate officers, or of the Commander-in-Chief. McDowell, leaving his column under the same circumstances, to consult Pope, the Court in his case adjudged committed a clear offense, and only omitted to punish for it from an impression that his motives were innocent. Porter remained, as he should, with his troops, and sent one of his aids, Lieutenant Weld, to Pope. That officer states, "about four o'clock on the afternoon of the twenty-ninth," he started on his errand. He bore a written and verbal message to Pope from Porter. The latter was "to the effect that General Morell would soon be strongly engaged; that there was a large force in front of us." The glance that he had of the written one showed him, he said, that it was to the same purport, "but much more minutely, with details"—what they were, he did not remember. He found Pope, "and delivered the message to him, both written and verbal," and asked if there was an answer. Pope told him, "Tell General Porter we are having a hard fight," and said, that "was all he had to send to General Porter." The witness wrote this down, and afterward delivered it in person to Porter. He further stated, that on the way to Pope he "saw General Hatch," who was in command of King's division, that officer, as Hatch said, being sick, and not present. That he gave Hatch both of the messages, as Porter had authorized, and asked him for an answer, and was told, "Tell General Porter that we have whipped the enemy, and are driving them," but soon added, Don't deliver that answer, but this, "Tell General Porter we have driven the enemy in the woods." (P. 129.) This also was delivered to Porter. With these facts in his possession, on what ground could Porter have supposed that Pope needed on his battle-ground Porter's column?

Who was best able to judge? Pope, who was on the site of the battle, and in command of all the forces engaged, or Porter, who was several miles distant? Had Porter not a right to consider that if his assistance was needed, a request, or order to that effect, would have been sent by Pope, in reply to his written and verbal messages by Weld? Pope had the right to demand his assistance. But he not only failed to do this, but even to intimate that he desired it. If the assistance was needed, and not asked, (and it is clear that it was not,) then one of these conclusions follows:

I. Either Pope designedly failed in his duty, or II., had not the intelligence to know (though on the spot) that Porter's corps was needed. But he is not blamed by the Judge-Advocate. On the contrary, (however it may excite surprise, or cause a smile with those who remember the disorganized army that fell back upon the Washington defenses, and its crest-fallen chief,) he tells us, "That it can not be improper to add, what the Record will sustain me in saying, that so far as light is shed upon the subject by the testimony, the Army of Virginia appears to have nobly performed the arduous and perilous work committed to its hands. Its campaign was brief, but marked by signal *vigor and ability*, and animated by a spirit which, shrinking from neither toil nor exposure, nor danger, bravely struck the enemy whenever and wherever he could be found." (P. 316.) The only way to account for so singular an opinion, is by supposing that the Judge-Advocate closed his eyes to all the evidence in the Record, except that of Pope, Roberts, and Smith, (a fault belonging to the whole of his review,) and also by supposing that the universal voice of the public upon the campaign, which literally filled the land, never found its way within the walls of his office. But it is strange, that when he was penning this eulogium and lauding "the signal vigor and ability of Pope," it did not occur to him, that it was possible the people would find in the fact, that when the President discovered the Capitol in imminent peril, he at once relieved the so much lauded chief, and about the second of September, placed the army under the command of Major-General McClellan, and on the fifth of the same month gave to Porter the command of eighteen thousand men, to guard the most important portion of the intrenchments around the city, and continued him in that position until the twelfth, when he ordered him to the command of his former corps, to which a new division was attached, in the army, with which McClellan, to his great honor and to the incalculable advantage of the country, and the safety of the Capitol and the Executive, fought the battles of South-

Mountain and Antietam—conclusive evidence that the President did not then share in the confidence of the Judge-Advocate in Pope, or in the truth of his eulogium, or participate in his present detraction of Porter.

II. But as the joint order, for the reasons already assigned, as long as McDowell and Porter were together, placed the command of their united forces in McDowell, his order was conclusive on Porter. To have disobeyed it would have been a high military offense. Did McDowell give an order, and what was it? The facts that he gave one, and what the order was, are conclusively proved by the evidence of Locke and Martin, before referred to, and which was not at all weakened, much less rebutted by that of McDowell.

III. Porter's "falling back," the Judge-Advocate says, was the ground on which the Court decided that there "was a violation of the joint order." (P. 308.)

I. The only proof urged to sustain the fact that there was a falling back is a note (which will be given hereafter) of Porter to McDowell and King, without date, but no doubt written and sent on the twenty-ninth, after those officers had left Porter's corps. At this time, Porter was, as before stated, authorized to judge for himself. That this was his right, McDowell having then separated from him, the Judge-Advocate nowhere contests. On the contrary, he admits that McDowell then ceased to have any rightful authority over Porter, and that he (Porter) was left "untrammeled," and empowered to decide for himself what was to be done under the joint order. (P. 307.) He not only makes this concession, but in another part of his review, as has been seen, he goes farther, and maintains that even McDowell present, Porter had the right, under the order, to act independently of him. In this latter opinion he is certainly mistaken, but in the other, clearly right. The order told Porter that "it may be necessary to fall back behind Bull Run at Centreville to-night," and that "one thing must be held in view, that the troops must occupy a position from which they can reach Bull Run to-night, or by morning," "and that if any considerable advantages are to be gained by departing from this order, it will

not be strictly carried out." The power, therefore, to judge whether departing from the order would produce "any considerable advantages" was given to Porter exclusively. He had the right to decide on that as fully as Pope himself would have had if personally present. Error in judging of it is no offense if committed honestly. The power, however, was made subject to this positive limitation, that it was not to be exercised so as to place his troops in a position from which they might not be able to "reach Bull Run that night or by morning." Every thing to be done was to be in subordination to that object. If to march in a different direction, or to attack the enemy, or to do any thing else, would probably hazard that end, it was not to be done. And who was to decide this? Porter. Had he acted without regard to that primary purpose, and by doing so had frustrated it, he would have violated the order, and been justly liable to punishment. Now, what evidence is there that in any thing he did, after McDowell left him, Porter did not decide honestly? His Generals and several of his other officers were examined, and they exculpated him in this, as indeed they did in regard to all the charges. Nor, as to this, did the Judge-Advocate attempt to prove the contrary by any one of them.

If, therefore, Porter had in fact fallen "back," he was empowered to do so if he really judged it expedient, looking to the positive injunction, as to Bull Run, or to "advantages" that he thought would result from it. This proposition, however, is not necessary to his vindication. For there is not only no proof that he did fall back, but positive proof that he did not. "Falling back," as the Judge-Advocate uses the term, means *retreat*. Did his troops fall back or retreat on the twenty-ninth? There is not a scintilla of evidence of it; nor does the Judge-Advocate offer any evidence of any fact that even tends to establish it. He not only substitutes surmise for proof, but, in favor of surmise, he rejects positive and uncontradicted proof.

The proof is this:

1. *Morell.*—He stated that he received an order from Porter, written in pencil, a little before sunset on that evening, and soon after, through Colonel Locke, a verbal message to the same effect, direct-

isositions to attack
le did so. That the
countermanded, be-
of the hour, as sug-
he added: "I was
ere I was during the
de his dispositions
g them, and said,
d the night." (Pp.

ras produced, on the
he Judge-Advocate,

: I wish you to push
orted by two others,
ers; the regiments
undred yards, and
section of a battery,
battle works well
enemy are said to be
Give the enemy a
r troops advance.
J. PORTER,
eral Commanding."

roof this, that Por-
thinking of "the
imself) and staff"!
such to the special
itable Judge-Advo-
rther stated, "I re-
Porter an order to
re I was," in line of
front of the enemy,

s, Locke, and B. F.
troops remained in
of the enemy, all the
th. Locke said that
until the next morn-
the question, "was
, answered no." (P.
of the Government,
dge-Advocate, and
lly relied upon for
as asked by him,
y such display of the
nake it necessary, in
treat before them?"
d no means of know-
ed back from that
was for some proper
nderstand at all what
not receive any im-
retreating from the
hat we were making
el the enemy in that

direction, and, having found him, that we
had moved back for some other purpose
and, not knowing about the orders to the
General, I remained under that impression.
(P. 113.) Is it not then passing strange,
that with this clear proof, the Court should,
as the Judge-Advocate says they did,
"and justly," have found that Porter did
fall back, did retreat on that evening, and
in that way (the only one suggested)
violated the joint order? It can but be
accounted for as other gross errors can
only be by assuming the existence from
some cause aliunde of judicial and official
blindness. The only ground relied upon
by the Judge-Advocate is the following
note, heretofore referred to, from Porter
to McDowell and King.

" GENERALS McDOWELL AND KING : I
found it impossible to communicate by
crossing the roads to Groveton. The
enemy are in strong force on this road,
and as they appear to have driven our
forces back, the firing of the enemy having
advanced and ours retired, I have determined to withdraw to Manassas. I have
attempted to communicate with McDowell
and Sigel, but my messengers have run
into the enemy. They have gathered
artillery and cavalry and infantry, and the
advancing masses of dust show the enemy
coming in force. I am now going to the
head of the column to see what is passing
and how affairs are going. Had you not
better send your train back? I will communicate with you.
" F. J. PORTER,
" Major-General."

Waiving for the present, what however
is most obvious, that if Porter had withdrawn to Manassas, (his purpose when this
note was written,) the movement would
have been within the discretion vested in
him by the joint order, yet as the evidence
is clear, *that he did not so withdraw, but,
on the contrary, continued where he was
in front of the enemy*, when the note was
written, and until the morning to the
thirtieth, and then only marched under a
positive order from Pope, he could have
been found guilty of falling back or retreating upon the twenty-ninth, only upon the
hypothesis, that an *unexecuted* purpose is
the exact equivalent of an *executed* one.
In the view of ordinary minds, to do is
one thing, and to intend to do, another—

but with this Court and Judge-Advocate, they are in fact and in law identical, and Porter has been adjudged guilty of disobedience, not because he did disobey, but because he, for a moment, contemplated disobedience. There is no better way of meeting such reasoning than to state it. Like all palpable follies, it answers itself.

The Judge-Advocate asserts, however, that the purpose to "retreat," "most energetically," as he says announced in the note, "was promptly carried out substantially if not to the letter, because at between five and six o'clock, the accused was found at or near Bethlehem Church, surrounded by his troops, whose arms were stacked." (P. 308.) He omits, however, to inform the President, or even to allude to it, that the greater part of his troops, Morell's division, as proved by Morell himself, remained during the night, and, by Porter's order, where McDowell left them, in the immediate front of the enemy, and in line of battle, prepared either to repel or attack, as the occurrences of the night might require. That all the troops were not there, upon the point in question, proves nothing. The Judge-Advocate would seem to think that there was a retreat, if the whole corps was not retained at the spot—placed in solid column, standing erect, and with arms at the shoulder. But this is mere fancy. What witness proved a retreat in a military sense? Not one, whilst Morell, Locke, and B. F. Smith testified that there was no retreat, in fact, and no order given for one. Here again hypothesis is made to do more than take the place of proof—it is used to supplant it. The Judge-Advocate, conscious that the order from McDowell to Porter of the twenty-ninth, which Colonel Locke positively swears he received and delivered that afternoon, would be a full justification for Porter's not attacking the enemy, assails the witness. This he does, not by calling witnesses to impeach his character for veracity, or in any other respect, but by proving, I., by McDowell, that he did not recollect giving the order; II., by King, that he was not with McDowell (as Locke had said he was) when McDowell, as *stated by Locke*, gave the order. The reviewer says, that McDowell "declared that none such was sent by him." This is not so. He made no such statement—on the contrary, he studiously avoided doing

so. He but professed not to *recollect* having given it. King's evidence was to the same effect. He was only asked by the Judge-Advocate if he *remembered* being with McDowell about the time when Locke testified he received the order, and said that he did not. And to another question he answered, that he did *not remember* hearing McDowell give any such order that day. In his case, then, as in McDowell's, there existed but *a want of recollection*. Is this to destroy the evidence of a witness not otherwise impeached, who swears that the order was given? As far as there is proof, and as those who are acquainted with the parties, know to be the fact, Locke's character for veracity is as perfect as that of McDowell's or King's. Why then is his truth assailed, and their being mistaken even, treated as impossible? King admitted that he was sick on that day, and although he did not state what his disease was, yet, as he said, he was too sick to take part in the battle of the succeeding day, and was forced to leave his division to be led by Hatch; as his loyalty and gallantry are beyond all question, his sickness must have been severe. Certain diseases we all know (and King's may have been of that kind) produce listlessness and impair memory. And yet on this negative and wholly unreliable evidence, it is maintained by the Judge-Advocate, that no such order was given, and that Locke, the equal in virtue of McDowell and King, willfully swore false.

Mistake as to the fact to which he testified was impossible. If the order was not delivered by McDowell to Locke, then the latter knew it, and his testimony was designedly untrue. But, whether the order was in fact sent by McDowell, Locke positively swears he delivered it to Porter as coming from McDowell. No one contradicts this, either positively or negatively. To receive it as true, therefore, would seem to be unavoidable; but it is not so with the Judge-Advocate. He assumes, without charging it designed falsehood on the part of Locke in his statement, that the order was sent by McDowell, and then maintains that the other fact proved by him, the delivery of such an order to Porter, is to be rejected as untrue on the authority of the maxim, which, according to his reading, is "*falsum in uno, falsum in omnibus*," (it should be

"*falsus in uno, falsus in omnibus.*") De-
sirous, however, as he evidently was to
impeach the credibility of Locke, he could
not bring himself to charge him with
willful falsehood. And yet the maxim
has no application to any other. And it
applies there, because in such a case, the
very ground on which credit is given to
human testimony fails. You can not be
certain in such a case whether there is
truth in any part of the witness's evidence.
"Having (says the Judge-Advocate) been
discredited as laboring under a complete
misapprehension in regard to the first,
(the receiving the order from McDowell,)
this discredit necessarily attaches to the
second, (the delivery of such an order to
Porter,) and under the *maxim quoted*, his
entire statement falls to the ground." (P.
314.)

Mistake—"misapprehension," as to one
fact, the Judge-Advocate asserts—taints
the whole evidence of the witness, and
demands its rejection. It establishes,
therefore, in the sense of the maxim, according to his understanding of it, falsehood. If this was its true construction, in
how many cases could testimony be of any
avail? What witness but proves at times
to be mistaken, or to misapprehend some
of the facts to which he testifies? Human
memory often honestly fails — is human
testimony on that account to be rejected?
But if misapprehension as to a fact legally
and morally discredits every other portion
of the evidence of a witness, for the same
reason the misapprehension of the meaning
of a legal maxim, would deny to him who
entertains it any legal knowledge. The
misapprehension of the meaning of the
maxim quoted by the Judge-Advocate,
every student will see is clear beyond all
doubt. Its meaning is stated with his
accustomed perspicuity by Mr. Justice
Story, in the case of the Santissima, 7
Wheat. 338. "Where a party speaks to
a fact in respect to which he can not be
presumed liable to mistake, as in relation
to the country of his birth, or his being in
a vessel on a particular voyage, or living
in a particular place, it is extremely difficult to exempt him from the charge of
deliberate falsehood ; and Courts of Justice, under *such circumstances*, are bound
upon principles of law, and morality, and
justice, to apply the maxim *falsus in uno,
falsus in omnibus.* What ground of
judicial belief can there be left, when the

party has shown such gross insensibility to
the difference between right and wrong,
between truth and falsehood?" But yet
how unfair it would be to deny to the
Judge-Advocate even very distinguished
legal attainments! He so wished to get
rid of the fact fatal to his immediate purpose, the approval of the sentence against
Porter, that he was oblivious for a moment
of the true sense of the maxim or of the
moral principle on which it rests.

It is unaccountable also why the Judge-
Advocate did not call the President's attention to the positive statement by Porter
in his defense, that Locke delivered the
order to him. Did he doubt Porter's
truth? Did he think his statement false?
He could not. He must have known, or
could have informed himself, that in the
estimation of all who knew them, Porter,
as a gentleman, and man of honor, is in
every respect the peer of McDowell and
King and himself. It is no answer to this
suggestion, that Porter's defense is not
evidence. It is not legally, but it is morally.
Locke being confirmed by Porter, whose
veracity no gentleman will question, should
have saved Locke from the charge of perjury, so recklessly made by the Judge-Advocate.

But the evidence of Locke, after Mc-
Dowell and King were examined, is so
clear that it is impossible not to credit it.
After stating why he considered McDowell's message to Porter singular and important, he said that on that account "it impressed me very strongly all the way up to
the time that I gave it to General Porter."
That its character was such that he thought
no one should hear it but Porter, and that
he therefore "delivered it to him in an
under-tone," and that he had "*never forgotten* the messages or the incidents connected therewith." He also described
minutely where he found McDowell and
King. At the time he knew the former
well, but not the latter. And in conclusion
was asked this question, "Are you entirely
positive, as much as you can be of any fact,
that you did deliver to General Porter, on
the afternoon of the twenty-ninth of August, words which purported to be a message from General McDowell, to the effect
that General King was to be taken away,
and that he, Porter, was to remain where
he was"? and answered: "I AM POSITIVELY
CERTAIN OF IT." (Pp. 223, 224.)

It is not thought that there was a person present when this evidence was given, not excepting the Judge-Advocate, who did not fully believe it. It was impossible to do otherwise. The manner of the witness, his evident intelligence, the reason he assigned for his conviction, all united to challenge absolute confidence in his truthfulness and accuracy. To discredit him as to the fact of delivering the message to Porter, on the authority of the legal maxim quoted by the Judge-Advocate, is as cruel as it is legally absurd. With as much, indeed greater propriety, could the maxim be used to destroy the whole evidence of McDowell and King. The one is proved by Locke to have given the order, the other to have heard it given. No fair legal mind can doubt this. They say, they do not recollect the facts. The Judge-Advocate maintains "that, under the circumstances, this is in effect the same as positively swearing that the facts did not occur."

They then are found to have labored "under a complete misapprehension in regard to" them, and, being to that extent "discredited," the discredit necessarily attaches to "all the evidence," and under the maxim, "falsum in uno, falsum in omnibus," to use the Judge-Advocate's Latin, the entire evidence "falls to the ground." That an accusation of falsehood against these officers, on that ground, would be most unjust and disreputable to him who should make it; all will agree, and none, it is supposed, more decidedly than the Judge-Advocate. And yet such an imputation is cast by him on Locke, on that very ground and no other. The topic is too unpleasant to be further considered. But finally, on this specification, how the Court could find it against Porter is incredible. It averred only disobedience of Pope's joint order.

Whether that existed or not was best known to Pope. Porter's conduct was all before him. He was informed of every thing that he had done under the joint order. And yet with this information, in no part of his evidence did he state or intimate that the order had not been obeyed. All that he said on the subject, or that the Judge-Advocate could induce him to say, was not that that order was not obeyed, but the subsequent one of half-past four of that day. At the time this last order was received, the proof is clear and uncontra-

dicted, that Porter was doing every thing required by the joint one.

Neither Pope nor any other witness testified to the contrary. And yet the Court found the specification true. Such a finding under all the circumstances can serve but to disparage their intelligence in the estimation of the public.

THIRD SPECIFICATION.—FIRST CHARGE.

Disobedience of the half-past four order of the twenty-ninth of August. The order was as follows:

"HEADQUARTERS IN THE FIELD,
"August 29, 1862, 4.30 P.M.
"MAJOR-GENERAL PORTER: Your line of march brings you on the enemy's right flank. I desire you to push forward into action at once on the enemy's flank, and, if possible, on his rear, keeping your right in communication with General Reynolds. The enemy is massed in the woods in front of us, but can be shelled out as soon as you engage their flank. Keep heavy reserves and use your batteries—keeping well closed to your right all the time. In case you are obliged to fall back, do so to your right and rear, so as to keep you in close communication with the right wing.
"JOHN POPE,
"Major-General Commanding."

I. It will be seen that this order assumes that Porter's line of march under the joint one would bring him "on the enemy's right flank."

It directs him, therefore, when he gets on that flank, to attack it "at once," and if possible the enemy's "rear." To do this last, the flank was necessarily to be first turned. So that the order with reference to both the flank and rear attacks, was intended to depend on the contingency of Porter's march under the previous order, bringing him "on the enemy's right flank." As this, however, necessarily involved the line of the enemy's march, as well as that of Porter's, and neither he nor Pope could control the former, Pope could not have been certain when he issued the half-past four order, that Porter would be brought by the route he was pursuing under the joint order on the enemy's right flank. Pope therefore could not have designed (the words indeed of the half-past four order negative such a design) that Porter was to attack, unless his march brought him on that flank of the enemy. If it should bring him on the enemy's left or centre, then the order from necessity became inoperative.

II. Where then, pursuing as it is admitted he did, the route prescribed by the joint order, was Porter's command when he received that of half-past four? The proof is all one way. He was not on the enemy's right flank, but in his immediate front, and where he was in full force. Not only then was the order inoperative, but to have attempted in that position of his troops to have marched them toward the enemy's right flank with a view to attack that, and, if possible, his rear, would not only have failed, but almost certainly have been followed by serious if not fatal consequences to his command. What was the fact? Was the enemy in his front, and in force, when he received the half-past four order?

I. At what hour did he receive it?

The Judge-Advocate on this, as well as on every other point of doubt, decides so as to prejudice Porter. The rule is otherwise in every system of civilized jurisprudence, and this is believed to be the first case in which it has been uniformly departed from.

Facts have not only been disregarded, inferences, the wildest and most uncharitable, indulged in, but the best established legal principles, without even a sophistical reason to excuse it, totally repudiated. But when did Porter in fact receive the order? The Judge-Advocate admits that in regard to this, "there is a decided conflict in the testimony." He seems rather inclined to conclude for himself, that it was received about half-past five o'clock. And he suggests that "it may be that after carefully considering all the circumstances, the Court felt that the explicit and intelligent statements of Captain Pope and his orderly, fortified by the corroborative evidence of Generals Pope, McDowell, and Roberts, were not overcome by the opinions of the five officers examined on the part of Porter. (P. 309.)

But what is the evidence?

1. *Captain Pope* of General Pope's *staff.*—He says that he supposes that the distance between Pope and Porter, when he got from the former, the half-past four order, was "three miles," and swears that it was in Porter's hands "by five o'clock." On cross-examination, he admitted that he fixed the hour when it was handed to him, by Pope, from the time stated on the face of the order. He did not profess other knowledge of it. He described the road he took to get to Porter, and said that he returned by the same road. (P. 57.)

2. *Charles Duffer*, the orderly.—He fixed the distance between the two Generals, not at three, but at "about *five* miles, as near as he could judge from traveling the road." This is the distance that the Judge-Advocate adopts, discarding, in that respect, what he calls "the explicit and intelligent statement of Captain Pope." He says that Pope "rode as fast as his horse could carry him, and had but about five miles to travel, and yet, according to the theory of the defense, that he did not arrive until sunset, or half-past six, he was two hours on the way," and then asks, with an air of triumphant logical confidence: "Is it credible that a staff-officer, bearing an important order in the midst of a fiercely contested battle, would have traveled at this rate, and this too when he was conducted by an orderly acquainted with the road, and encountered no obstacle? Is it not much more probable that but a single hour was occupied, and that, in point of fact, he arrived at half-past five?" (P 309.) He thus rejects as to the time of arrival, as he had done as to distance, Pope's evidence, and adopts that of the orderly, and yet tells us, that the statements of both, though materially conflicting, were adopted by the Court as being "explicit and intelligent." He also says that these statements were "fortified by the corroborative evidence of Generals Pope, McDowell, and Roberts." How this could be, when the statements were contradictory of each other, it is not very easy to comprehend. But let that pass. What is the supposed corroborative evidence?

1. *General Pope.*—"I know that an aid-de-camp, riding *rapidly*, could go from the field of battle to Manassas Junction, or to any point west of Manassas Junction, within an hour, by going at *speed.*

2. *Roberts*, the disinterested prosecutor of Porter—he says that he was present when the order was issued, and gives it as his opinion that it should have been delivered " in half an hour or less, as orders are generally delivered on such occasions."

3. *McDowell*.—He agreed with young Pope as to the time and place, when he says he saw the witness. Neither of these officers even profess to know when the order in fact was delivered to Porter, nor at what rate of speed the messenger traveled, nor the character of the road he passed over; and yet their opinions are gravely relied upon as confirming the statements of the messenger and his orderly, although they vitally conflicted with each other. And their statements and their supposed corroboration are held sufficient wholly to rebut the positive proof of five witnesses of admitted intelligence and unquestioned integrity, who were present when the order was delivered, and concurred as to the time.

That this would be manifestly unreasonable if the evidence of the two was the same, and if neither was contradicted in any material fact, every impartial mind will agree. But in this instance, it is the more obviously unreasonable since Pope is contradicted as to other material facts than the hour at which he says he delivered the order, and, II., Duffer, the orderly, disproves the facts on which Pope and Roberts, and the Judge-Advocate, base their opinions. Captain Pope stated first, that after giving the order to Porter, he returned by the same road by which he had arrived; second, that no one pointed out to him the road on his return, except his orderly.

In both these particulars he is expressly contradicted.

1. *By Lieutenant Weld*.—In his evidence in chief, he says, that he carried, on the afternoon of the twenty-ninth, an order from Porter to General Pope, and adds, I " got back *after sundown*—I think it was about a quarter to seven o'clock when I got back, as near as I can recollect." That General Pope's messenger to Porter (admitted to be Captain Pope) " *came afterward*." " I was told to show this messenger the direct road back to General Pope. I did show it to him, and described it, and even drew on a piece of paper the

road I had taken, which I afterward found out was not the direct road; there was a little variation in it. He could not see the road; he did not seem to understand where the road was, where it crossed the railroad. Some one then told me that I had better go and show him where the road was, and I went up to the railroad with him, and pointed out the road that I had taken." " He started on it." (P. 180.)

2. *Lieutenant George T. Ingham*, Aid-de-Camp to General Sykes.—Was present, he said, when the order was delivered to Porter, and knew Pope, the messenger " *it was after sunset*." That Pope did not remain " there more than twenty or twenty-five minutes at the outside." That after he had left, the witness was sent by Porter to recall him. " I rode on pretty rapidly, and I found Captain Pope had got between a quarter and a half-mile. There were several officers on the road, and I had to ride up close to Captain Pope to see who he was, it was *so dark at that time*." He further stated that Pope, on starting to return, did not take " the Sudley Springs Road, the road he finally took," but " was bearing off down the railroad, toward Manassas Junction, and that he then told him to take the left-hand road, and that then Lieutenant Weld (the former witness) went down to the road with Pope, to show him which road to take." (P. 199.) It will be remembered that Pope had sworn that he had returned by the same road that he had come, and that no one had pointed out to him any other.

3. *Major-General Sykes*.—He was present when Captain Pope delivered the order to Porter. It was " as near sunset as I can remember; *certainly*, within a little before sunset, or after sunset." (P. 177.)

4. *Locke*.—He witnessed the delivery, and said it was " between sundown and dusk." (P. 136.)

5. *Montieth*.—Was present, knew Pope, and says he delivered the order about " sundown." (P. 127.)

All this evidence, however, is rejected by the Judge-Advocate, and, as he tells us, by the Court, although the witnesses were with Porter when the order was delivered, saw it delivered, and concurred in stating that it was about sundown. Their statements are at least equally "explicit and intelligent" as Pope's and his orderly's, but they are passed over, and theirs adopted.

II. Nor does the corroborative evidence relied upon in support of the latter amount to any thing. It consists of mere opinion, whilst the rejected evidence was positive statement of facts, made on personal knowledge. When the order could have been delivered, in the judgment of Generals Pope and Roberts, and how long it would take a messenger to go from the point where he saw McDowell to Porter's tent, can be but mere opinion. General Pope says an hour Roberts says a half-hour; in no exigency, does he fail, the Judge-Advocate. But to carry the message within either an hour or half-hour, they unite in saying that speed was necessary. Pope says it could be done within the time he named, "by going at speed"—Roberts, in his "half-hour or less, if carried as orders are generally carried on such occasions." Whether it was in fact carried "with speed," or as is "generally" done, neither ventures to say. The Judge-Advocate presumes "speed," from the character of the message. He can not believe it "credible that a staff-officer" could be more than an hour in performing such a duty. In his view, it is nothing that five intelligent and honorable witnesses swear positively to a later delivery. He, and, as he says, the Court, adopts the statements of Pope and his orderly, not only not corroborated in any manner, but expressly contradicted in the very material fact of the roads traveled coming or returning. The reasoning of the Judge-Advocate is, that the messenger did what he professes to have done, because he should have done it.

He also maintains, in the support of his hypothesis, that Pope "rode as fast as his horse could carry him." How fast that was, depended on the character of his horse and of his orderly's, and the nature of the road. To suppose all horses go at the same pace, and that their speed is irrespective of the nature of the road, is not exactly logical, if experience is to be considered. And in this case, too, to conclude that actual speed was had in the sense in which the term is used by Generals Pope and Roberts and the Judge-Advocate, is to disregard the evidence of the orderly. It is apparent that the Court, who alone examined this witness, (he was produced by the Government, after Porter had "rested his case,") would like to have had him prove that great speed was used in the transmission of the order, but in this they failed. He said: "Sometimes we were on a trot, sometimes on a walk, and sometimes on a canter, going about as fast as we thought our horses could travel." (P. 208.) He was then asked: "How much of the way did you gallop?" And answered: "That is more than I can tell you. We went as fast as we could from the nature of the road, and as we thought our horses could travel." He was further asked: "Do you remember whether you trotted or walked, or galloped the most of the way?" and replied: "*We had to go a good deal of the way quite slow, on account of the road being very bad, rough in places.*" The Court, unwilling to abandon their purpose, asked this additional question: "Did you gallop any at all?" And were answered: "Yes, sir, we did." I recollect galloping *some*, in other places we had to go *quite slow*. (Pp. 209, 210.)

The speed, therefore, required, in the judgment of Generals Pope and Roberts, for the delivery of the order by five, or five and a half o'clock, was not used, unless to travel "a good deal of the way *quite slow*," as proved by the orderly, and not disproved by young Pope, is to go with *speed*. It is not only true, therefore, that the preponderance of evidence shows that the time of the delivery of the order was about sunset, but that there is not any reliable evidence to the contrary. Even, however, if the first part of the remark alone was correct, the Court should have found the fact, that the delivery was at that time. They had neither the legal nor moral right to find it otherwise. Where witnesses are equally intelligent and fair in character, the testimony of the greatest number is to prevail. The probabilities of mistake (designed mistake in such case being impossible) are less likely with many than a few. The Court, consequently, in pursuing the course attributed to them by the Judge-Advocate, violated both legal and moral principle. In addition, however, to the distinct proof of the five witnesses, which was made to yield to that of the two; though one of the two was positively contradicted, and the evidence of the other but served to confirm that of the five, there was before the Court, in regard of the transmission of other orders in which no error was intimated, evidence that strongly confirmed that of the five. It is this:

The important and urgent order of three A.M., of the twenty-ninth, (p. 28,) for the corps to march at dawn of day, was not delivered till six A.M., (about two hours after dawn,) though the distance was only *five* miles. The one of seven P.M., of the twenty-sixth, (p. 154,) not till eleven P.M., and another of four A.M., of the twenty-seventh, (p. 153,) was also four hours in its delivery, though the distance was but six miles. And the one of eight-fifty P.M., of the twenty-ninth, (p. 7,) dispatched to and from the same point as the four-thirty order, was six hours and forty minutes in its delivery, the distance being but four miles.

Neither of the officers who bore those several orders were reprimanded by Pope for delay. Nor could they have been, justly. The roads were very bad, and comparatively unknown, and the horses much broken down by prior hard work. Speed, of course, was impossible. It can not be necessary to pursue the inquiry further.

The order, then, having been received about sundown, or, as General Sykes says, "*certainly* within a little before sunset, or about sunset,"

I. Was it obeyed? And

II. If not, why not?

The proof is distinct, that the moment it was received, Porter sent an order to Morell, who was in the advance, to attack the enemy.

1. *Locke* says, Porter handed me the order, and "very soon afterward ordered me to ride up to General Morell, and direct him to move forward and attack the enemy *immediately*, and to say, that he would be up himself right after me." (P. 136.)

2. *Morell* says, that soon after sunset, Locke "came to me with an order from General Porter to make the attack, (he had been preparing for one under a prior

order.") "I told him, (and I think in my message to General Porter, I spoke of the lateness of the day,) that we could not do it before dark." (P. 147.) This order was afterward, and in the judgment of Morell, properly, countermanded. He thought that the day was too far advanced, and the enemy too well and strongly posted in the front, and in too great force to justify the attempt. In this opinion all the officers in the command concurred. Colonel Marshall, as will be seen presently, most decidedly.

The Judge-Advocate states, that "by the inaction" of Porter's command, and by its "falling back," (a charge before refuted,) "the enemy had been so far encouraged in their advance, that at this hour, the front of (Porter's) column was not separated from the advance of the rebels by more than a mile, or a mile and a half," and that "little time therefore was required to make the attack." He fails, however, to inform the President, what is evidently true, that the joint order of the twenty-ninth from Pope, was designed to prevent the junction of Longstreet's corps, supposed to be twenty-four thousand, and Jackson's twenty five thousand. That it was for that purpose, that Pope, by that order, united the commands of McDowell and Porter. Before McDowell separated from Porter, he had read General Buford's note to General Ricketts, as appears by his evidence. (P. 83.) That note was dated at half-past nine o'clock A.M. on the twenty-ninth, and stated that "seventeen regiments, one battery, five hundred cavalry, passed through Gainesville three quarters of an hour ago, on the Centreville road. I think this division should join our forces now engaged at once. Please forward this." (P. 84.) He also said the regiments averaged 800 men. Buford, at the time he sent this note, was at Groveton, about four miles from Gainesville. The proof is most conclusive that it was Longstreet's corps that Buford referred to, and that it was that corps which was in the immediate front of Porter. If it was, as is supposed, the purpose of the joint order that an attack should be made to prevent the junction of Longstreet and Jackson, by the blended commands of McDowell and Porter, it should have been made at that time. Instead of this, McDowell, who being the senior in rank, had the control of the whole force, retired with his own corps, taking with him a division of Porter's, (King's,) and repaired to a distant point, which he was several hours in reaching, and where he was beyond a supporting distance from Porter. This is alluded to under the present head, to confirm the statement before made, that prior to his withdrawing and reducing by more than one half, the force which Pope had assigned for the attack, and leaving Porter with an enemy over double his own force in front, he never gave Porter an order to make the attack. This conclusion is necessary to exempt McDowell from the imputation of reckless folly, gross military ignorance, and a disregard of what he must have known was the design of the Commander-in-Chief. It was in this condition of his force, that Porter received the order of half-past four. And as already appears, he gave orders, without the least delay, to make the attack, and abandoned the purpose afterward, because of the approach of night, which made it, in the judgment of Morell, as well as in his own, impossible to make an effective one. It is asserted by the Judge-Advocate, that there was not an "earnest or vigorous effort on the part of (Porter) to obey the order." Morell says, as has been already seen, that the moment he received Porter's order through Locke, he proceeded to place "the men in position to make the attack;" And Locke says, that the moment Porter received the order, he carried one from Porter to Morell to attack, "at once." The Judge-Advocate assumes that there was but a small force in Porter's front, and rests for his assumption principally upon the testimony of General Roberts. It is sufficient to say, in relation to his evidence, and to show how totally unworthy of consideration it is in this particular, that he does not pretend to have seen Porter's position on that day, later than "about one o'clock." He could not therefore have seen the position, or had any information of the strength of the enemy in Porter's front, later than that hour. Nor does he pretend to have been nearer to it, at any time of the day, than "a mile and a half." He says, too, "I could not see his command, there were woods intervening," nor could I "see his immediate front." (P. 215.) And yet, although it was literally impossible that he could have any information to justify it, he gives it as his opinion that there was

"only a cavalry force with some light artillery," in Porter's front. And yet, more strange is it, that the Judge-Advocate adopts this opinion in preference to the testimony of Major Hyland, attached to Colonel Marshall's regiment of skirmishers, and who was eight hundred or a thousand yards in advance of Morell, and near the enemy, of Lieut. Stevenson, of Colonel Marshall, Morell, and of every other officer examined, who was with Morell's command on that evening. Under the circumstances, his criticism upon the testimony of Stevenson, that "he was a young man with limited experience," is amusing, when it is remembered with what confidence he relies upon the testimony and opinion of young Pope, Smith the orderly, and Roberts, with his admitted ignorance of the facts upon which he gives his opinion. The reliable evidence upon the point which was rejected by the Judge-Advocate is, however, conclusive.

1. *Major Hyland.* — He belonged to Morell's division, and was on the evening of the twenty-ninth in "the front of it." That his regiment was at the time "employed as skirmishers," "from about one o'clock of the afternoon of the twenty-ninth, until daylight of the next day. That the Twenty-second Massachusetts and Berdan's sharpshooters were placed on our left in the evening." That the enemy "commenced forming between two or three o'clock," in our front, "there appeared to be two columns of them." The witness indicated the position of his regiment, and the enemy on the map, which was before the Court. That no portion of the enemy was on the left of his regiment. That he knows of their forming to attack (Porter's force) during the day. He "could hear the commands plainly as if forming in line, and the movements of their artillery coming into position." On cross-examination by the Judge-Advocate, in answering this question with reference to the number of the enemy, "Can you state how many thousands, or divisions, or regiments?" he answered: "I could not state the number of thousands, or divisions. I judge, from the movement and from the commands given, that there *was a very large force* indeed, *probably a larger force than we had.*" He reported the force to Colonel Marshall, his commanding officer. He further stated that

he thought it "*was sufficient to have made a successful resistance to General Porter's entire corps.*" Although unable to state with accuracy the number of the enemy, he yet added, that "from what information I had, and from what I could get from the other officers, I thought their force was *very heavy indeed.* I should think there were probably ten thousand troops in front of us. Judging by the columns of dust that I also saw coming from the same direction." And in reply to a question by the Court, he stated that in his opinion "the strength of the enemy," in Morell's front, was increased by the "strength of their position." (Pp. 174–176.)

2. *Stevenson,* of the Thirteenth New York Volunteers, Marshall's regiment. On the twenty-ninth, he went on horseback "from ⸱the left flank of General Pope's army to the position then occupied by" his regiment. That the distance was "between a mile and a mile and three quarters." That he was almost an hour in traveling it, and reached his regiment "between one and four o'clock in the afternoon." That when he got there he could "*see the enemy,*" and "judge him to be about between twelve and fifteen thousand." That he could "see his forces of different arms, infantry and artillery," and could see that "he was receiving reinforcements."

3. *Colonel E. G. Marshall,* of the Thirteenth New-York Volunteers, was with his regiment on duty with General Morell's division, on the twenty-ninth. "About one o'clock, I was detailed by General Porter to go with my regiment across an open country and a ravine, to some timber that was facing our line of battle, and deploy skirmishers to find out the position of the enemy, and any thing else that I could find out concerning them." They were "*a very large force, and they were drawn up in line of battle as they came down.*" After describing the manner in which the enemy approached, and saying that he deemed it so important, that Morell should know their position, that he was unwilling to trust his orderlies or others with messages, he said that he repaired himself to Morell to confer with him "concerning the enemy." "This was about dusk." Upon hearing from Morell, that he had orders from Porter to attack the enemy, and

finding that Morell was much troubled concerning it, and that he "asked my advice," says, "I told him BY ALL MEANS NOT TO ATTACK, THAT IT WAS CERTAIN DE-' STRUCTION FOR US TO DO SO; THAT I for one did not wish to go into that timber and attack the enemy. Their position was a very strong one, and they were certainly in force at that time, TWICE AS LARGE AS OUR OWN FORCE, ALL OF GENERAL POR- TER'S CORPS." He also said, "that if we had attacked them, I felt that it was CERTAIN DESTRUCTION." "Afterward, at dark, I was sent for by General Porter, and questioned very stringently with reference to the enemy; and my remarks to him were the same as I am now making, and as I made to General Morell." (Pp. 189, 190.)

The force of the evidence of this last witness, the Judge-Advocate attempts to avoid by asserting, that he was "largely influenced in forming his opinion from the clouds of dust which (the Judge-Advocate says, not the witness) may have arisen as much from the movement of ambulances and wagons as from the march of troops. The witness, in answer to this question of the Judge-Advocate, "Did you make your estimate of the amount of that force *principally* from the extent of the line as indicated by the *clouds* of dust, or had you other means than that of judging?" said, "My estimate was made *mostly* from the *length of time,* which they were coming down—there appeared to be artillery and infantry—and the time that we were at-. tacked, and also from what I had seen of the enemy's dust prior to going on this duty, and the *length of their lines,* as much as I could see of it in our front."

There is no foundation, therefore, in fact, for the criticism of the Judge-Advocate. Of the intelligence, integrity, and patriotism of this witness, the Judge-Advocate does not even insinuate a doubt. Nor does he question his military capacity. He was a Captain in the regular army, and for his ability and gallantry was made Colonel of his regiment. His gallantry was greatly displayed in the then recent battle of Fredericksburgh, where he was severely wounded. The Court repaired to his chamber, where he was confined, and there took his testimony. To discard the evidence and opinions of this witness, and of Hyland and Stevenson, and to adopt the ridiculous opinion of Roberts—ridiculous, because founded in ignorance, as he admitted, of the facts—is an insult to the understanding.

It being then clear, that it would have been madness in Porter to have attacked the enemy, who were in his front, at sunset on the twenty-ninth, and equally clear, that to have done so would not have been justified by the 4.30 order, but, on the contrary, would have been a violation of it, as it directed him to attack the "enemy's flank, and if possible, his rear;" let us see whether, when he received it, he could have made such attacks. At that time there was, as proved by Marshall, and the other witnesses referred to in Porter's front, a force of the enemy twice as great as his own. To have reached their flank he must have marched in front and to the entire distance of the enemy's line. Their force consisted of infantry, cavalry, and artillery. With this force they could have assailed him in every foot of his progress, and readily have attained a position in his own rear, which must have ended, in all human probability, in his annihilation, and if so, in the destruction or capture of Pope's army. But, in addition to this, the country over which he would have had to pass was so broken and filled with ravines and timber, that it would have been impossible, in the darkness which then prevailed, to have moved his infantry in any thing like order, and utterly impossible to have moved his artillery. To have left the latter behind him would have subjected it to certain capture, and would have been a direct violation of the order, as that directed him on his march to "keep heavy reserves and use your batteries."

The Judge-Advocate says, "It may be admitted, and perhaps the *testimony requires the admission* to be made, that falling upon the enemy on the afternoon of the twenty-ninth, (Porter,) would have encountered both difficulty and danger," but adds the very original remark that "difficulty and danger in time of war are daily and hourly in the category of the soldier's life. Their presence should be for him, not a discouragement, but an inspiration. To grapple with them should be his ambition; to overcome them, his glory." (P. 312.) Without meaning to call into doubt the capacity of the Judge-Advocate to judge what would be a soldier's ambition or "glory" in such an exigency, it is certainly not discourteous to him, to say that such soldiers as Hyland, Marshall, Morell, and Porter, who saw the difficulty and danger, are judges more to be relied upon. In comparing in this particular the Judge-Advocate with Porter, no disparagement is intended of the former. When he shall have been in as many battles—shall have conducted himself with as much skill and valor—shall have won the same grateful applause—have received such signal manifestations of approval from the Government—have done so much to fill the whole measure of a soldier's ambition and glory, he will then, and not before, have a right to be heard with respect, as to what, in any particular instance, should be a soldier's ambition and glory. Let us, however, examine what was the extent of the "difficulty and danger" which the Judge-Advocate admits to have existed. In considering this question, the Judge-Advocate accepts the least and rejects the most satisfactory evidence. He relies on the opinions of Lieutenant-Colonel Smith and McDowell, formed in ignorance of the country to be passed over, or of the length of the march, and of the force of the enemy in Porter's front. That such opinions are entitled to no weight, must be obvious to every fair mind. In a court of justice, where the principles of evidence are apprehended and impartially applied, they would be promptly rejected, and the counsel who endeavored to maintain them lose reputation with the bench and bar. The reliable evidence is this:

1. *General Reynolds.*—He had passed over the country on the twenty-eighth with his command, and says, he found it "so broken, wooded, and obstructed that I had to turn into a road leading along the railroad from Gainesville to Manassas Junction, and finally marched on that road in one column, around to Bethlehem Church, toward the old battle-field of Bull Run, late in the evening." That the country between New-Market and Groveton was "very broken by ravines and wooded; I will state that *I know that from having passed over it on horseback that night*, from somewhere in the neighborhood of New-Market over to the Warrenton Pike, near Groveton." In his judgment, a command could not have passed over that country in force, with artillery,

in proper order to face an enemy, if it had to "move in the immediate presence of an enemy."

On cross-examination by the Judge-Advocate, he was asked: "You say that a command with artillery, etc., could not have passed over the country between New-Market and Groveton, in the immediate presence of the enemy: was not the ground equally bad for the enemy as for General Porter? And if the enemy could take position there, why could not General Porter's troops have taken position against them?" And answered: "*It was impossible to manœuvre troops over that country.*" They could take position there, of course, and they could be attacked in position by troops. *But it would have been very difficult to have got artillery up through that broken country, and a very disadvantageous attack would have been made.*" He was afterward asked: "Did you or not pass over the country stretching from your left toward General Porter's position, on the twenty-ninth, while on the march from Gainesville toward Manassas Junction?" And answered: "*Not with my command.*" "Did not the enemy, in attacking the left and rear of General Pope on Saturday, the thirtieth of August, pass with artillery and infantry much of the country that General Porter would have had to pass over on the twenty-ninth to attack the right of the Confederates?" He replied: "*I think not;* I think it had gotten in, as it were, between that broken country and our position on that day, occupying a ridge which crossed the turnpike there, and having the broken country behind him. Because I manœuvred the day before, the twenty-ninth, all over, up to that broken country, and got partially on that ridge with one brigade." The Court, evidently unwilling to abandon their desire to show that Porter could have made the attack, not satisfied with this answer, put to the witness this additional question: "Could so large a force as passed around your left on Saturday, have done so without passing over a long distance toward where General Porter was?" And received this answer: "He had the Warrenton Turnpike open for him, and by coming down that turnpike, he filed in off that turnpike, as I supposed, though at a different point, through this broken country. He had that advantage

in coming down and occupying this ridge." (Pp. 170–173.)

2. *Morell.*—This inquiry was made of him: "Seeing your own position and that of General Porter's command, so far as you knew it, at the period of the day in question, between sundown and the gray of the evening, and seeing all that you knew and believed of the position of the enemy at that time, please to state whether an attack by General Porter's command upon the right flank and rear of the enemy at that time was possible." And answered: "The only attack we could have made at that time would have been *directly in front.* The firing of which I spoke was far to the right, and at that time we could not have got there. The troops of the enemy in front of us were under cover in the woods. If we had moved forward we would have gone over this open space, where our men would have been exposed to the fire of the enemy, without any possibility of effectively returning it."

"Such being the case as to a movement on your left to attack the enemy by flanking him on his right, please to state whether you could have passed through the woods on your own right in any good order to attack the enemy in that direction." "I doubt whether we could have got our artillery through, *even by daylight.* We might have passed through the woods with our infantry, but *not in any fighting order at all.*"

"Would it have been possible to carry your artillery through that wood by night?" "*No sir,* I think not." (P. 147.)

The force of this testimony was not attempted to be weakened by the examination of either the Judge-Advocate or the Court. The intelligence of the witness, and his well-known high character, would have rendered such an effort fruitless.

3. *Marshall.*—"Was it possible, (he was asked,) without the greatest danger, for General Porter to have made a movement to his right to attempt to reach and attack Jackson on his right?" "No sir; it was *impossible to have done so.* In the first place, it was impracticable to cross the country in that position during the day. Again, we would have been obliged to have whipped the very force in front of us, large as it was, to have got there,

and it was very doubtful if we could have done it."

He also said, that if Porter had "attempted the movement," the enemy "would have attacked our flank." The Judge-Advocate did not think it prudent to examine the witness at all upon the point, but the Court were less cautious. They asked whether, "from the position of the forces, both those of the enemy and our own, would the march of General Porter, to reach the right flank of Jackson, have been direct or circuitous?" And were answered:

"*It would have been circuitous, through a broken country.* If he had endeavored to go the most direct route, it would have been through a broken country. But I do not conceive that it was *practicable* for him to have gone that route. I think that in order to have acted upon the enemy he would have had to go back the same route we took the next morning in retreating." "Not practicable, (the Court further inquired,) because of the character of the country or the position of the enemy?" And were answered: •

"Because of the broken country; it was rocky, and then a part of it was very heavily timbered, and it would have been *impracticable to have carried artillery through there,* besides being fired upon and met by the enemy in our front." (Pp. 191–193.)

There was other testimony to the same effect, but it is unnecessary to give it in detail. It is submitted with perfect confidence that this evidence is conclusive to show that the order of 4.30, which alone forms the subject of this specification, could not have been, at the time it was received, executed. In this opinion, *all of Porter's officers who were acquainted with the condition of things concurred.* Under these circumstances, if Porter had made the attempt to execute the order, and had been, as he certainly would have been according to this testimony, defeated with great, if not total loss, he would have committed a most serious military offense, for which he should have been, and no doubt would have been, held responsible and severely punished. If that had occurred, too, judging from the treatment he has received, no one can doubt that the failure of Pope's campaign would have been attributed to such rash and unmilitary conduct.

How ridiculous it is to reject the evidence of the above-named officers; and how insulting to the intelligence of a reader, to ask him to put faith in the opinions, not statements of facts, of Smith and McDowell, given in admitted ignorance of the facts which rendered a compliance with the order impracticable. Smith's opinion is based, as he states, "on the fact that that portion of the country over which (as he understood it) the corps of (Porter) would have moved upon the enemy, "*was sufficiently practicable to enable the enemy, as they did, to make a similar movement on our left on the next day.*" (P. 77.) The Italics are the Judge-Advocate's. Not only did he omit to inform the President, what in fairness he should have done, of the evidence here given, but to advise him that the fact on which Smith's opinion was formed, was not true. That Reynolds had proved that the enemy's movement on the thirtieth *was not over the ground which Porter must have passed on the twenty-ninth* to have attacked their right flank. And McDowell's opinion was based upon the same misapprehension, and only upon what (as he said) was his "knowledge of the country, derived principally from having gone over the railroad from Manassas to Gainesville in a car, or on a locomotive, which gave me but little idea of it, as I was engaged whilst going over with matters which prevented my paying attention to the country." And upon several other facts, for the most part immaterial, and unknown to him except upon hearsay. (P. 93.) The Judge-Advocate seeks to aggravate Porter's supposed offense by stating with entire confidence, that if the order had been obeyed it "would have secured a triumph for our arms, and not only the overthrow of the rebel forces, but probably the destruction or capture of Jackson's army." He states that this would have been the result if a vigorous attack had been made by Porter "at any time between twelve o'clock, when the battle (between Pope and the enemy) began, and dark, when it closed." And for this he refers to the opinions of Pope, McDowell, Roberts, and Smith, "all of whom participated in the engagement, and were well qualified to judge." This confidence is somewhat amusing, when it is remembered that Pope and McDowell never achieved a victory, Roberts no one thought could ever achieve one, and Smith was a volunteer of but a few months' standing, and never before under fire.

But, waiving this, how totally immaterial are those opinions when the proof is clear to the dullest comprehension, that the attack directed by the order, when that was received, could not have been made, and when there was no prior order stated in this specification, or either of the other two under the first charge, directing an attack to be *made* at all.

FIRST, SECOND, AND THIRD SPECIFICATION OF THE SECOND CHARGE.

These will be considered together. They are framed under the fifty-second Article of War, which embraces " misbehavior before the enemy." They charge Porter with such misbehavior on the twenty-ninth. It will be seen that this concedes that there was no order from Pope to make an attack on that day. This charge has been substantially anticipated. It has been proved conclusively, that no attack could have been made, except with the almost certain result of serious defeat, if not destruction. Either of which would have been fatal to Pope. Nor is the fact true upon which the Judge-Advocate relies, that during the time from twelve o'clock to sunset on that day, a severe battle was raging between the rest of Pope's command and the enemy, within the hearing of Porter. On the contrary, the officers, all of them who were with Porter, agreed in stating that the battle appeared to be mainly with artillery, and at some miles from his position. That Porter had no reason to believe, and did not believe that an attack by him was necessary for Pope's safety or success, appears by his order to Morell, brought out on the cross-examination of the Judge-Advocate, and received about sunset, or a little before sunset. (P. 150.) That order informed Morell, " *the battle works well on our right, and the enemy are said to be retiring up the pike.*"

This reply has assumed dimensions greater than was anticipated. It was found unavoidable however, from the necessity of giving in detail many portions of the evidence. The object of the writer was to expose the injustice done Porter by the Judge-Advocate—to rescue him from the influence of the reputation of that officer ; and to demonstrate to the public the gross wrong done him by the Court, and unconsciously, as is thought, from misplaced confidence, by the President. In this he can not have failed. He thinks that in the public judgment, when the case is fully understood, the finding of the Court will be considered to be without explanation, except upon the ground of mental imbecility or blinding prejudice. The first certainly did not exist. The latter is believed to be established.

With a view to avoid this last conclusion, one which the Judge-Advocate appears to have anticipated, he ventures (and in so doing, greatly compromises his legal reputation) to say: " It is not believed that there remains upon the Record a single ruling of the Court to which exception could be seriously taken." Those rulings are on pages 17, 21, 24, 39, 41, 51, 71, 96, 214, 221.

There were several others which Porter's counsel considered erroneous, but omitted to except to them, in order to save time, and from their then having no hope, that any thing they could say, would change the rulings. These involve two propositions—first, whether it is competent for a witness to state his opinion upon the meaning of orders written or verbal; and second, whether, when the prosecution, with a view to show the alleged criminal *animus* of Porter, had given in evidence his telegrams and conduct, on the twenty-seventh, twenty-eighth, twenty-ninth, and thirtieth of August, it was not competent to Porter, in order to disprove such *animus*, and to show his loyalty and his determination to do his full duty before getting, and after coming under Pope's command, to offer in evidence his telegrams, and conduct on the twenty-fifth, twenty-sixth, thirty-first of August, and the first, second, and third of September telegrams, constituting a series, of which those offered by the prosecution, were a part.

I. Without stopping to inquire if a decision on this head was correct, which either admitted or rejected the evidence, all will agree, that to admit it in some instances, and reject it in others, can not but be erroneous. And that is just what was done by the Court. When Porter asked the opinion of a witness, the question was objected to and overruled. When the Judge-Advocate, or any member of the

Court, asked such a question, though objected to by Porter, because the same privilege was not allowed him, the objection was overruled, and the evidence received. The Record will show that this was uniformly the case. Its evident partiality and palpable injustice render further remarks unnecessary.

II. To exclude statements and conduct made and occurring a day or two before and after the date of those relied upon to establish Porter's criminal *animus* when offered to explain the latter, and to disprove such *animus*, is an error so gross, that it is amazing how the Court, though not lawyers, could have fallen into it, and more amazing how the Judge-Advocate could sanction it. The admissibility of the evidence is proved, clearly, it is thought, in Porter's protest, Appendix No. 1.

But notwithstanding the finding and sentence of the Court, and its approval, and the malignant and bitter assaults upon him, before and since, Porter will stand unharmed through the potent power of truth and the public judgment. The latter ever cheers the patriot, and sooner or later frustrates the aim of the demagogue, and palsies the arm of the traitor. In addition, too, to this support, he possesses in himself one even yet more potential. He is self-sustained in the consciousness of innocence, and conviction of duty fully performed.

What shield against injustice is more invulnerable? It abides with the injured at all times and everywhere; consoles him in adversity—enhances his prosperity. It is an adjunct to truth and justice, an antidote to falsehood and calumny, and in the end is certain to bring their authors before the public in full relief, to be the scorn or the jest of the honest.

The friends of Porter, therefore, need feel no further concern for him. He and his accusers stand for judgment before a just and enlightened tribunal, and what fair mind can doubt the issue?

But we must all feel deep solicitude for the country, now passing through a dreadful crisis. No people was ever subjected to a more perilous one. But this solicitude is not because we doubt the result, if the Government is true to its own duty. If it is, the danger will soon be over, and who can doubt that it will be? If keeping a single eye to the extinction of the rebellion in conducting the war, they discard mere party, cast off intrusive and ignorant politicians, observe in the loyal States, where the ordinary course of justice is unobstructed, all the constitutional guarantees of personal liberty, recognize every individual right, regard freedom of speech and of the press, (a freedom which the people will never suffer to be impaired,) restrain the excessive enthusiasm or madness of misjudging officers, instruct them that it is their duty to war with the rebel enemy alone, and to observe in so doing all the humane rules of the modern laws of war, suffering no harm to be done to private property, nor the appropriation of it for other than military purposes, cease to foster the incompetent, and in an enlarged and enlightened statemanship, sword in one hand and the olive-branch of forgiveness, conciliation, and compromise in the other, (the enemies are our brothers, and we but seek to bring them back to the common household,) all will ere long be well again. The rebellion now so shaking the land, like as

> "Ocean's mighty swing,
> When heaving on tempest's wing,
> It breaks upon the shore,"

will have subsided, and before the historian shall have written its history, even its vast wrecks of material wealth, and its vaster and more distressing wrecks of former harmony and affection, will have been forgotten in the magnitude and universality of the blessings in which the whole land will then be rejoicing.

Nor portentous of destruction as is the black cloud that lowers over us is there serious ground for despondency, much less despair. A beneficent Providence can not design so to affect us, and, through us, the world. Great as our national sins may have been, and deserving of punishment, as they no doubt are, it can not be that such a Being will strike a nation like ours out of existence. Protected and regulated freedom is so important to human happiness, that, if we may, with reverence, speculate on such a subject, it must be within the scope of Heaven's design to secure it to all. And in the past what has contributed more to that result than our example? With institutions resting as their sole foundation on individual liberty, we have by its inherent and almost magic power prospered as never people prospered before; so unexampled and striking has this been, that all nations looked at us with wonder—the rulers of some with envy—the oppressed, everywhere, with hope and gratitude. Is such an example to end forever? Believe it not. If, however, in the inscrutable dispositions of Heaven, it is so to be, and we are hereafter to live but in memory, of one thing we may rest assured, that that dire calamity will not be caused by the fulfillment of the object of this rebellion. That object, even ostentatiously and shamelessly avowed, is not to vindicate and maintain freedom, nor even to rescue human slavery as it at present exists, in some of the States, from the hazard of a possible early overthrow, but to extend and perpetuate it through all time. In the very City and State of their nativity, and which for so many years were guided, benefited, and honored by the wisdom and presence of Mason, Jefferson, Madison, Marshall, and Washington, in defiance of all the doctrines which they inculcated, and shocking the world by their astounding and iniquitous degeneracy, it is proclaimed, without rebuke, and no doubt by the authority of him who sacrilegiously holds out Washington as his model, that the main object of the rebellion is to establish a Confederacy which will be "A DISTINCT REACTION AGAINST THE WHOLE COURSE OF THE MISTAKEN CIVILIZATION OF THE AGE." "THAT FOR LIBERTY, EQUALITY, AND FRATERNITY THEY HAVE DELIBERATELY SUBSTITUTED SLAVERY, SUBORDINATION, AND GOVERNMENT. THAT HOWEVER AMONG EQUALS EQUALITY IS RIGHT, AMONG THOSE WHO NATURALLY ARE UNEQUAL EQUALITY IS CHAOS." "THAT THERE ARE SLAVE RACES BORN TO SERVE, MASTER RACES BORN TO GOVERN." Such are the fundamental principles (what a profanation of the term!) which, addressing themselves to the universe of man, they say: "We inherit from the ancient world, which we lifted up in the face of a perverse generation, that has forgotten the wisdom of its fathers." (Spirits of the great departed, let us hope that you do not hear the vile calumny!) "By these principles we live, and by their defense we have shown ourselves ready to die; reverently we feel that our Confederacy is a God-sent missionary to the na-

tions with great truths to preach." "And who hath ears to hear let him hear."*

No, no. Through such an instrumentality God will never work our destruction. He libels Deity who for a moment credits it. An honest man might as soon be suspected of effecting an end by fraud, perjury, or murder.

There is then no reason for despair. The rebellion will not triumph. Its fate is already sealed. The lamentations over its anticipated early death are heard in the wailings of the conspirators. The much-boasted army of Lee has been arrested in its recent invasion of Maryland and Pennsylvania by the unsurpassed bravery of the Army of the Potomac, handled with consummate skill by Meade, the gentleman and soldier, and driven back, with terrific slaughter, to its own impoverished and desolated Virginia, stealing away at night, under the cover of darkness and storm, in the demoralizing fear that the arm of the Union was approaching utterly to crush them. Vicksburgh and Port Hudson have fallen, and the States of Louisiana, Tennessee, Kentucky, Western Virginia, Maryland, and Mississippi, are ours, and the Father of Waters knows no standard but the Stars and Stripes. The very leader of the conspiring band, for years the plotters of the treason, is losing heart. In the beginning of his wicked career, he ridiculed the power of the loyal States, and vauntingly threatened them with the feeling of "Southern steel" and "the smell of Southern powder." Now, he stands conscience-stricken and appalled. He sees, and well he may, the finger of God in their dreadful reverses, and calls upon his deluded and ruined followers "to unite in prayer and humble submission under God's chastening hand." He tells them that they are to attribute their trials and afflictions to their forgetfulness of Him, and to their "love of lucre," (what an admission for proud chivalry!) which had "eaten like a gangrene into the very heart of the land, converting too many of them into worshipers of gain, and rendering them UNMINDFUL OF THEIR DUTY TO THEIR COUNTRY, TO THEIR FELLOW-MEN, AND TO THEIR GOD." †

To their country! How could he have

---

* See *Richmond Examiner*, May, 1863.
† Davis's Fast-day Proclamation of the 25th of July

ever even dreamed that forgetfulness of duty to country, to fellow-man, and God would not meet with the chastening hand of heaven? Davis, the educated and often honored child of the Union, over and over again pledged by solemn oath to support it, is at last aroused to a sense of the guilt of oaths violated and duty to country forgotten, and on his knees implores the forgiveness of Omnipotence. What stronger evidence could there be that despair of success of his criminal career now fills his very soul?

It has, too, in its very form of government, the seed of its own certain dissolution —secession is made the vital principle of its organism. No government is certain of living a day, but, on the contrary, is certain of a speedy death under such chronic and ever active disease. Whilst it defies cure, it is certain, sooner or later, to produce death. And before a single nation has recognized its legitimate existence, the disease has manifested its fatal nature. GEORGIA and NORTH-CAROLINA have already disputed the Confederate authority, and threatened withdrawal under the acknowledged theory of secession. So alarming has the threat become, and so obviously fatal to the Confederacy, that notwithstanding its constitutional recognition of the right, it has been denied in serious debate in their Congress, and the insubordinate members menaced with the exertion of the central military power. Our own downfall then, if ever, is not to be now. The rebellion will be put down. If not by force, as it may be, if our rulers are equal to the emergency, and as it is believed it will be, it will fall through the very feebleness of its form of government. Fall it will. Fall it must, and the United States be restored to the condition in which our fathers left it. A nation of which its citizens can speak with an honest pride as being destined to make "the world its debtor by its discoveries of truth and example of virtuous freedom."

APPENDIX.

I.

WASHINGTON, D. C., December 26, 1862.

WITH all proper respect for the ruling of the Court on Wednesday, refusing the accused the right to give in evidence the telegrams and messages he then offered, dated before and after the twenty-ninth of August, (that is to say, from August twenty-second to September first, 1862,) he begs leave to enter on its proceedings this protest.

The accused is charged, among other things, with having disobeyed the several orders stated in the specifications of the twenty-seventh August, 1862, twenty-ninth August, 1862, (4.30 P.M.,) and twenty-ninth August, 1862, (8.50 P.M.,) and the prosecution has endeavored to prove that such disobedience was by design, because of a fixed purpose on the part of the accused not only to coöperate with the General in command in the existing campaign, but to fail in his duty in that regard.

With this view, certain papers, being a part of the same series of telegrams with those rejected, were offered by the Judge-Advocate, not objected to by the accused, when the purpose for which they were offered was stated, and received by the Court.

And with the same object the opinions of the witnesses, Roberts and Smith, founded, as they said, on what they represent to be the manner and conversation of the accused, and also on what the first said he heard from another that the accused would fail the Commander-in-Chief.

In the words of the Judge-Advocate, this evidence was produced to show the *animus* of the accused toward his chief, and in that aspect was admitted by the Court. The accused respectfully maintains, that if evidence of that description, for such a purpose, be admissible, (as he concedes it is,) it is equally admissible, and is his right, to show by his conduct just before, at, and after he came under the command of General Pope, by what he did and by what he said, orally or in writing, that the asserted purpose—the alleged ANIMUS—is wholly untrue; but that, on the contrary, his real purpose—his real *animus*—from the first to the last, was to do his whole duty to the utmost of his ability, and render his General and his country all the aid in his power.

If the prosecution had contented itself with exhibiting the orders in the specifications which he is said to have disobeyed, and given evidence of the fact of disobedience, the accused is advised that, even then, the proof which the Court has ruled out should have been received. But when, not content with that course, it has attempted to prove his mental purpose—to fathom his mind—to show that from personal grudge to his General, or other cause, he designedly disobeyed such orders, he is advised that the evidence rejected is clearly admissible.

The general rules of evidence are the same in Courts-Martial as in other Courts. They are based on principles of universal application, and which, as experience has demonstrated, are best calculated to ascertain the truth. One of these, as well settled as any known to the law, is, that where a mental intent with which an act is done is in issue, the acts and declarations of the party a few days before, at, or a few days after the time when the intent is charged to have existed, bearing on such intent, may be given in evidence by either party. This is a familiar rule in cases, among others, of acts of alleged bankruptcy or insolvency, change of residence, and of many acts of alleged fraud. In the first, whether the act charged as an act of bankruptcy is one or not, often depends on the intent with which it is done; and what the party did before or after is constantly admitted as legitimately illustrating the actual intent.

In the *second*, Whether a man has changed his residence often, also depends on intent. He may have removed, to remain permanently or temporarily; and what he has done or said before and after removing is allowed to prove or disprove intent.

In the *third*, Whether the imputed fraud was perpetrated or not, often depends on intent unexplained. The mere act itself may appear criminal or innocent. It is the purpose which gives it its actual character, and this purpose may be shown by either party, by acts and declarations of the person charged before and after the period of the impeached act. This principle, I am advised, is fully settled, not only in all the elementary writers on evidence, but by the Supreme Court of the United States in, among other cases, that of Wood *vs.* United States. (16 Peters, 362.)

And it is respectfully hoped that the Court will, on further consideration, see the justice of the rule. Its justice is strikingly illustrated in this instance: the accused is charged with the dishonorable, traitorous purpose of having disregarded the orders of his Chief, to gratify some supposed personal dissatisfaction with him, wholly reckless of its consequences to his country. He is charged with having caused the defeat of our arms, and hazarded the safety of the Capitol, under the same degrading impulse. One of the witnesses has sworn, without objection from the Judge-Advocate or the Court, that a deceased officer of chivalrous character and spotless patriotism had declared to him, before the date of either of the orders, that the accused would fail his Chief. Another has stated, also without objection, that his conduct and manner in his presence were such that he was satisfied that he was a traitor, and that nothing but the fear of human laws prevented his killing the accused on the spot. This evidence was offered and received to show his *animus*—his intent. Proudly conscious of his innocence, and knowing the baseness of the calumny, he did not object to its introduction, being perfectly willing to let it all go for what it is worth. But to deny him the right, after it is received by the Court, to meet it by proving what is wholly inconsistent with it—acts of duty about the same period, orders, and messages, having no possible purpose but a faithful discharge of duty to his Chief and his country —it is submitted is a violation of the rule of evidence, and is to deprive him of the very best and most persuasive proof that the nature of the accusation admits of.

To show that he was not a traitor, he desired to establish constant acts of duty immediately preceding and succeeding the acts which he is charged to have done traitorously. To show faithfulness to duty to his Chief, he desires to prove, as the rejected evidence does, that to get to his command, and after he reached it, he did every thing that diligence, zeal, ardor, and all the skill and ability which he possessed enabled him to do to assist his Chief in every possible way, and at every possible hazard, so as to render his campaign a successful one.

Your ruling puts this out of his power, and, respectfully protesting against it, he can do nothing further than to submit it to your more mature consideration. (P. 253, 254.)

F. J. PORTER, Major-General.

II.

In addition to the propositions embraced as mentioned in the text, other gross errors characterized the rulings of the Court. 1. As will be seen, (p. 21,) this question was propounded to Pope.

"If, as you have stated, you were of the opinion that the army under your command had been defeated, and in danger of still greater defeat, and the Capitol of the country in danger of capture by the enemy, and you thought that these calamities would have been obviated if General Porter had obeyed your orders, why was it that you doubted on the second of September whether you would or would not take any action against him?"

The witness declined to answer it, "as not being *relevant* to this investigation." The Court was thereupon cleared, and when opened, the Judge-Advocate stated its decision was, "that the question was *irrelevant!*" Porter submitted a protest in writing. The Court was again cleared, and after some time was opened, and Porter told that his protest would be held "under advisement until" the next day. On the next day, the protest was read by the Judge-Advocate, and is as follows:

"The witness having, in his examination in

asters of the army under
ia, in August last, to the
) obey all or some of his
ited that he was of the
'ders might have been
o far as the prosecution
dence that such disobe-
e prosecution has endeav-
the accused is advised
e question just ruled out
y relevant and legal, but
o show that the recollec-
such his examination in
d upon; and that he for
charged the alleged dis-
used; because it was the
t only to doubt whether
on in relation to the mat-
ime as a grave offense on
; and his determination
ould take such action, or
acts not only admissible
that at the time to which
did not believe there had
ience on the part of the
respectfully requests to
d on the proceedings of
xclusion of the question

RTER, Major General."

said: "The witness re-
of the Court to answer
in the protest just read."
) objection.
red- and after some time
Advocate announced the
he witness have permis-
tion. When the witness
for *irrelevancy*, his ob-
after the protest is heard
and he requested to be
question, it was decided,
is known in the opinion
t to allow him the per-
t had no authority to re-
testimony, the result of
e the relevancy or irrele-
o the decision of the wit-

II.

is adopted by the Court
iestion put by Porter to
24.)

V.

, whose evidence was
rter, was asked by one of
y with a view to impair
*feelings toward General
lly.* The gross indelica-
ed another member of the
d it was then withdrawn.

Porter by his counsel protested against its withdrawal, because as it was apparent that the
member of the Court propounding it was under
the impression that such feelings existed, it was
Porter's right to have the truth of the imputation tested, and the right of the witness to be
permitted to exonerate himself from it. But
the Court decided that it should not be answered, and neither the question, nor what occurred
in relation to it, were permitted to appear in the
Record.

V.

In the Reply, (p. 11,) it is said that the
writer did not know what, if any thing had been
done, for Lieut.-Colonel *Thomas C. H. Smith.*
He has since ascertained that he was appointed
a Brigadier-General, to date from the twenty-
ninth of November, 1862. The Court was opened on the twenty-fifth of that month. On what
day the appointment was made he is not informed, but it must have been after he gave this testimony against Porter, on the eleventh of December, in the same year, as at that time he
stated himself to be a Lieutenant-Colonel, under
a commission dated the twenty-fourth of August, 1861. As he admitted upon his examination that he had never been in any army before
that date, and never received a military educa-
tion, and never was in a battle prior to Pope's
Virginia campaign, and there being nothing to
show that he displayed there either scientific
knowledge or conspicuous valor, it must be true
that his promotion to the high rank of General
was not a reward for gallant service in the field
or distinguished military ability. But looking
to the time when he gave his evidence in Porter's case, and the character of that evidence,
and his conduct in publishing and circulating
his testimony and Pope's, and Roberts's only,
without any other part of the proof, it is left to
the reader to decide for himself to what cause it
is to be referred.

VI.

The Judge-Advocate considers as immaterial
the testimony of Porter's "former services and
character for faithfulness and efficiency as an
officer," although he admits it to be "FULL AND
EARNEST," because such evidence, he says, "is
held to be entitled to but little weight except in
doubtful cases," and to no weight when "it
comes into conflict with evidence that is both
positive and reliable."

That no such evidence as the latter was given
against Porter the reader has seen in THE REPLY.
He will also have seen that the case made
against him by the Government, in view of an
impartial and fair mind, was not even a doubtful
one. It is due, however, to Porter, that it
should be known how strong were the testimo-
nials to his former "faithfulness and efficiency"
by those who had known him longest and best.

1. *Major-General Burnside.*—"I have never
seen any thing to lead me to think that he was

any thing but a ZEALOUS, FAITHFUL, AND LOYAL OFFICER." (P. 181.)

2. *General Reynolds.*—"I have had opportunities to judge of General Porter's conduct, and I have always considered him AN ENERGETIC, FAITHFUL, AND DEVOTED OFFICER." (P. 170.)

3. *General Morell.*—"I do not think that he *ever failed* to do his duty." (P. 149.)

4. *General Sykes.*—He was asked, did you ever see in Porter "any slackness to do his duty, any evidence of a disposition to fail his commanding officer or his country," and answered:

No; I never have. General Porter is an officer whose zeal is so well established, that I hardly see the necessity of that question. I would like to add that General Porter's foresight, his providence for the wants of his command, and his attention to all the minutiæ of his command, are such and so great that I have often thought that he relied or trusted too little to the capacity of his division commanders. He seemed to do every thing himself. (P. 177.)

5. *General Butterfield.*—(Roberts had said that Major-General Kearny had told him that Porter "would fail General Pope.") Butterfield was asked whether he had had conversations with Kearny in relation to Porter, and said, "frequently," and "that he always spoke in the HIGHEST TERMS of General Porter, both as a BRAVE OFFICER AND A GENTLEMAN, AND AS A HARD WORKER." And Butterfield also stated for himself that he never saw in any thing that he did or said before, or when it was understood that he was to come under Pope's command, *any evidence of an indisposition to be faithful to General Pope and to his country.*

6. *Major-General McClellan,* under whose immediate eye Porter was during his command of the Army of the Potomac, said, that from what he saw of his conduct, or from what he heard him say, after he knew that he was to go to the assistance of Pope, he did, in his opinion, "ALL THAT AN ENERGETIC AND ZEALOUS AND PATRIOTIC OFFICER COULD HAVE DONE," and that he never had any reason whatever, at any time after he received notice that he was to go to Pope's aid, "TO BELIEVE THAT HE WOULD FAIL GENERAL POPE OR THE COUNTRY IN THE DISCHARGE OF HIS DUTY." (P. 196.)

VII.

The very material evidence on one point, of Colonel George D. Ruggles, was omitted in the Reply. It is here given.

He says that he was in a room of the headquarters of General Pope, at Fairfax Court-House, on the morning of the second of September, 1862, that Porter and General Pope were in the room, and that "I was engaged at the time, (he was Pope's Assistant Adjutant-General, and chief of staff,) writing orders for the position of troops." "While I was writing these orders, General Porter and General Pope had a conversation lasting about *twenty minutes.*"

"Whilst this time, studiously avoiding overhearing their conversation, I heard scraps enough of it to *know they were talking about the incidents of a few days previous.* At the conclusion of the interview, General Pope and Porter got up, and I heard *General Pope say to General Porter, that his explanations were satisfactory, with the exception of the matter* of the one brigade. I think he said, 'ENTIRELY SATISFACTORY,'" "though as to the word entirely, I can not swear positively." I think General Porter replied, "that (the brigade) can be easily explained," though I am not positive about his answer. He also stated that his recollection was, that he reminded Pope of this "conversation on the fifth or sixth of September, 1862." The Judge-Advocate, in order to destroy the force of this evidence, succeeded only in getting the witness to repeat what he had said before, that he was not positive in his recollection of the latter fact, stated by him, but that with regard to the other, Pope's telling Porter that he was satisfied, he was *positive and certain.* (Pp. 155, 156.) Nor did Pope, who was examined before in regard to it, deny it; on the contrary, he virtually admitted it. He said that he remembered that upon the occasion referred to, "I told General Porter that I had not reported him to the Department in Washington, and as matters stood, I thought *I should not take any action in reference to his case,* though I felt bound to do so in the case of Griffin." And when asked upon cross-examination whether he remembered the conversation between himself and Ruggles, testified to by the latter, he only said he had "*no remembrance* of it," but was "not *certain* that he had not," but was "very certain that Colonel Ruggles never stated thing of that kind to him," although he was "not prepared to swear *that he did not.*" The bearing of Ruggles's evidence upon the accuracy, if nothing else, of General Pope's testimony, and its conclusiveness of the fact, that Pope, when he was made acquainted by Porter with all the circumstances connected with his conduct under Pope's several orders, expressed himself satisfied, can not fail to be apparent to the reader, and fatal, in any fair judgment, to the finding of the Court.

www.ingramcontent.com/pod-product-compliance
Lightning Source LLC
Chambersburg PA
CBHW030858260626
47169CB00008B/2592